T0131684

INVASION
— OF THE —
WOODS

MITCH INTREPID

ARCHWAY
PUBLISHING

Archway Publishing books may be ordered through booksellers or by contacting:

Archway Publishing
1663 Liberty Drive
Bloomington, IN 47403
www.archwaypublishing.com
844-669-3957

Because of the dynamic nature of the Internet, any web addresses or links contained in this book may have changed since publication and may no longer be valid. The views expressed in this work are solely those of the author and do not necessarily reflect the views of the publisher, and the publisher hereby disclaims any responsibility for them.

Any people depicted in stock imagery provided by Getty Images are models, and such images are being used for illustrative purposes only. Certain stock imagery © Getty Images.

ISBN: 978-1-6657-2906-2 (sc)
ISBN: 978-1-6657-2904-8 (hc)
ISBN: 978-1-6657-2905-5 (e)

Library of Congress Control Number: 2022915952

Print information available on the last page.

Archway Publishing rev. date: 08/25/2022

I would like to dedicate this book to all my readers for their support with my most recent book, "Logbook Affairs", and the fine support team at Archway Publishing.

ONE

THE LARGEST EXPLOSION

I T WAS A WARM SUMMER night, early in September. The Minnesota residents were blessed with a slight breeze blowing out of the northwest on a perfectly clear night. The Chester Family lived in a quiet suburb to the southeast of Minneapolis. The neighborhood was built in the eighties with luxurious homes in the 3-4000 square foot range. The yards were well spaced, and the neighborhood was free of fences. There was plenty of woods throughout the area, which was home to many northern species of animals. Deer, turkeys, red foxes, and pheasant were a few of the more common inhabitants that roamed through the backyards. Rabbits, squirrels, and racoons shared the vast area as well. Scott went to bed around 7:30 pm. He was not feeling well, and his body was banged up good from the run-in with some bullies in the schoolyard. It was a tough first day at the new high school in Eagan. His mom was probably sleeping downstairs in the living room, resting in her worn and crooked recliner, wrapped up with Nana's old patchwork quilt. The TV might be on or off, it didn't matter. Very seldom did she watch an entire show. The light feathery curtains waved in front of his open window, allowing the 60-degree temperature to fill the privacy of his room. The metal screen kept the bugs out, yet welcomed the crisp clean air to frolic on in. His red display on his digital clock was the only thing visible inside the dark room, the alarm set for 6:40 am for the second day of school. The moonlight illuminated the curtains with the silhouettes of the oak tree branches wavering within the fabric. Long black shadows of the branches were spread across his shiny pinewood floor. Crickets and tree frogs broke the silence of the dark woods. An empty laundry basket rested next to his pile of dirty clothes from the weekend. His headset lay hanging off the head of his bed, his nightly sleep aid to initiate sleep before the music ended. The night was slowly elapsing towards midnight. He was in a deep sleep, dreaming about the old days, fishing with his dad and Uncle Billy up in the north woods. Suddenly, he was rudely awakened by a loud explosion, the biggest noise he had ever heard in his 14 years. Some items fell off his nightstand and landed on the hardwood floor. A couple of glass marbles rolled under the bed. The house shook with a scraping noise, and the neighbors' windows buckled from the aftershock. The floor trembled beneath the bed as it seemed to have taken a hop. **What the hell was that**? He lay in bed for a few minutes looking up at the ceiling, wondering of the possibilities. He had experienced a couple overhead lightning strikes in the past, but this was ten times louder, maybe more. There was not any rain in the forecast for days and the moon illuminated the clear night sky – he knew that thunder only happened when it rained. There was no commotion for several minutes following the high energy noise, this ruled out something like an airplane crash. Did he imagine it, maybe the tail end of a bad dream? Mom didn't seem to be stirring downstairs. The house was not on the verge of collapse. After lying there for an unknown amount of time, he slowly drifted back into a deep sleep. It was going to be another big day for him tomorrow.

Hours later, there were blue flashing lights illuminating the walls in the hallway. He slowly awoke and went to the open bedroom window all blurry eyed. He parted the soft lightweight curtain to one side. Officer Reynolds was talking in a low voice to his mom down below his window. She was in her white housecoat and nervously smoking a Lucky Strike. Her pink satin nightie was barely visible from beneath, just enough for the gentleman in uniform to take notice. The moon light reflected off her bare beautiful skin. Her silky legs were exposed from the knees down. The smell of soap and perfume filled the air. Scott remembered that officer from the church picnic several weeks ago. He and Mom seemed to hit it off well back on that warm summer day. In the community park, they sipped cold lemonade and reminisced about days gone by. The picnic was attended by dozens of parishioners. The event was filled with lots of activities for the kids. The blue charcoal smoke smelling of burgers, brats and dogs rose from the grates of several stainless-steel grills, and a live Bluegrass Band called the "Sinners" kept the crowd's attention. Even Father Medeiros was kicking up his heels, sipping on one cold beer after another, mingling with the congregation. If was a fun day to be had by all.

Now, the two adults were facing out into the woods and Officer Reynolds was talking with a serious business-like voice. Mom had put on the back porch light after seeing the two policemen searching the woods with their black mag lights. Several moths were already fluttering in circles around the dusty globe. A cicada buzzed along its secret flight path at the top of the trees. The officer's deep voice went forth with an explanation, "The only thing I could see was a large crevice in the forest floor towards the back of your property. I am thinking it was an earthquake of some sort". Scott's mom, Cheryl Chester was conversing with the tall officer. "We don't have any earthquakes in Minnesota Jake, do we?" He replied in a quick snippet, "With all the fracking that has been going on out in the western part of the state, Mother Earth is more unpredictable than ever". "Well, I guess" replied Cheryl. "I hope our gas prices come down soon, seems like the Middle East is sucking the money from our wallets. How is this situation in my backyard going to be taken care of?" Officer Reynolds answered, "That's quite a deep hole. I will talk with the appropriate group in the morning, and see to it that the Parks Department eventually fills it in. In the meantime, my partner is taping the area off, to keep the neighborhood kids the hell away from it! They could break a leg if they fell into it, worse yet, the walls could cave in on them. Should be fixed up in no time though. Keep a watch on it. If you find any damage to your home in the days ahead, I recommend you get your insurance man out here. My partner Dave will slide a copy of the police report under your back door when we finish up here, in case you have a claim. For now, have yourself a good rest of the night". Cheryl asked if the gentlemen would like to come in when they were done. "I'm afraid not Cheryl, our shift is coming to an end, and it's been a long night for us. We had to arrest a couple of juveniles that wanted to see who had the fasted Toyota in Eagan. They gave us quite a chase". He thought about taking up the offer after his shift once his partner left for home. *No, he knew that was not an option.* He was a family man devoted to the church and his marriage. Some dreams weren't meant to ever come true. Dave had turned off the blue lights on the patrol car, so as not to startle any neighbors in the quiet suburban neighborhood. After all, it was close to 3 am on a weeknight. Scott could hear what sounded like a large group of people gathered out in the woods. They were talking in low voices, possibly another language. He could not make sense of it, must be some neighbors gathered in a group. He scanned the whole area out back, from one side of the window to the other, the cheeks of his face pressed into the screen. The smell of the musty metal webbing filled his nostrils. There were no other people anywhere around. They would have surely had flashlights of some sort. Officer Dave was returning to the woods from the side of the house. His narrow flashlight beam panned back and forth, and he hugged a roll of yellow crime tape under his arm. Cheryl replied, "Thanks Jake, I appreciate you coming out here tonight, that was a very frightening noise! I never have experienced something so loud in my life". She dropped her spent cigarette to the cement patio and squashed it with the toe of her pink slipper. She returned into the house through the screen door in the back, getting one more peek at the tall handsome officer. A long strand of hair slid on to her cheek. The flimsy door closed with a pop from the tension of the spring. She closed the heavier door behind it and bolted the latch.

The tall officer returned to the woods, to witness his partner Dave tying off the final stretch of yellow tape. Jake could see Dave's flashlight cutting through the darkness. A well-worn path led to the area of interest, which snaked past the Chester's compost pile. The full moon reflected off the still pond over towards the north side of the property. The only sound was the steady chirping of the crickets and maybe a few tree frogs, a sign of the Fall season shortly ahead. These gentlemen could not hear the voices that Scott was hearing from up in his quiet room. There was a warmth coming from the crevice, with a little bit of mist rising a few inches above the ground. The heated soil beneath was being exposed to the cool Autumn air at the surface. The slice into the earth measured close to 25 feet long with the widest center area around four feet across. Loose soil seemed to have fallen into the center from the steep edges. Jakes partner exclaimed, "I've never seen anything like this around here"! Dave was the most recent recruit with the Eagan Police Force, and Jake enjoyed having him as a partner. He was knowledgeable about many topics, always professional and willing to learn. He even had a few jokes every so often to share with his partner. Dave interrupted the silence again with his young higher-pitched voice, "Brings back memories of California in my childhood life. We had plenty of quakes, big and small, but they usually shook for quite a while. Seeing a break in the surface was a rare event, other than what the media showed on the television. Mrs. Chester claims there was just one loud bang, and then a deafening silence. Well, there is no sign of a fire, and I do not think the hole is very deep. I think we should cruise by in an hour or so, just to check on things. I would hate to see the woods catch on fire, that would affect a lot of these nice homes in the neighborhood. Maybe there will be some aftershocks". Jake agreed and both the officers climbed the hill to return to the squad car out in the driveway. The only sign of life was the early morning newspaper guy randomly throwing rolled up newspapers outside his car window, leaving a thump on the neighbors' driveways. Jake remembered the days when he delivered the Pioneer Press. It was an early honor in life to have a paper route. The newer recruits would start out meeting at the main paper drop with a fresh white canvas tote bag with a long reflective orange handle, that could be proudly worn over the top of their head. This enabled them to ride a bicycle or a skateboard while distributing the newspapers. By the end of its tenure, the bag would turn gray from the black newspaper ink, the handle would fade and become tattered and frayed. Permanent neck damage from the Sunday newspapers was always a possibility. Nowadays, the routes were consolidated with some night owl adult driving swiftly through the neighborhoods for hours on end. The customers would never meet this person, monthly billing takes place through the mail. The delivery man turned his old rusty jalopy up a side street just as the officers came into sight, his face seldomly seen by anyone. The red taillights and the rumbling engine noise slowly faded off into the distance. Dave wondered if the car would even pass an emission test. The officers entered their vehicle. Jake looked in the rearview mirror, just as the red taillights of the Chevy disappeared around the corner. The interior smell of their squad car was of coffee and a hint of stale fast food from the quick lunch after the Monday meeting, held back at the headquarters. Empty coffee cups and paper debris were stuffed into every crevice, mostly up on the dash. It was Dave's obligation as second in command to clean the car up after their night shift. They sat in the cruiser for a short while and completed their report as the central computer screen lit up their faces. Young Dave turned to Jake, "Isn't it strange that we have had no other calls to the station about the loud noise"? The senior officer answered. "Well, it may be part of the story. I knew Cheryl's husband pretty well, we graduated high school together. Mike lost his life in Afghanistan earlier this year. It seems his wife likes to drown her sorrows out. I smelt liquor on her breath tonight, and I see her down at the liquor store quite a bit on my way to work. A good-looking lady, but she seems like she is 'out there'. It is just her and the boy. Maybe she exaggerated the volume of the noise a little bit in her alcoholic haze, who knows". Dave replied, "Well, if there was a shift with the plutonic plates deep below the surface, it could produce quite a snapping noise with many repercussions. I am just surprised there were no other people convening in the street discussing the event. Hey, the Joe in my cup is cold. I think I'm ready to refresh my morning coffee, what do you say"? Jake agreed. Something caught his attention in the rearview mirror though. With a knee jerk reaction, he unsnapped the leather strap over his revolver and rested his hand on the cold steel. A small bicycle with a dark dressed person was rapidly approaching from where the newspaper guy disappeared a few minutes ago. It was coming right towards them, the silhouette growing in size! The bike quickly turned before reaching the base of the driveway and continued on, making a large figure eight in the middle of the street away from the streetlight. There was the sound of a young girl laughing, and some sort of ticking noise that matched her speed. Jake flung the driver side door open and looked to the street. This bike was travelling at a speed faster than any child could pedal. The shadow of the bike raced ahead of the girl; an affect caused by the corner streetlight. Just then, the bike slid on its side and whacked against the ground. There was a scraping noise, metal against pavement along with what sounded like a canvas duffle bag dragged across the asphalt. The canvas was probably her skin though. The ticking noise abruptly ended, and a young girl's voice could be heard sobbing in pain and embarrassment. Dave had just exited the car and looked back as Jake was running toward the scene to help the child, reminding the officer of his own daughter. Dave noticed a tall person in a white gown of some sort running for cover behind a hedge across the street. The young girl rolled on her back at the edge of the yard looking up at the night sky. As Jake grabbed her small body to lift her, he was stunned. It was some sort of Paper Mache doll with a powder white face. It had bright red lipstick covering her lips and her eyes were closed. The blank stare clothed in the dark outfit sent a chill through his body. Suddenly a blue and red glowing ball rolled out her right pocket. Jake gently laid the doll back down in order to grab the bright object. He just missed picking it up as it rolled down the sloping street, picking up speed every second. Jake's pace began to speed up to a jog, but he was losing the battle. His police equipment and keys shook on his utility belt. He resecured the gun strap on the holster. The ball found its way to the nearest sewer drain and disappeared out of sight. As the officer peered into the iron grate from a standing position, the hole in the ground lit up with blue and red light, there was a young girl's voice laughing from deep down in the darkness. As Dave approached his partner from a distance, the glowing object extinguished, and the laughing stopped. "What are you looking at boss"? "Oh nothing, I saw an object that looked like an electronic ball or something that flung out the girl's pocket, but it's gone now". They walked back to the bicycle lying in the street, Officer Dave shined his flashlight off towards the hedge, nobody was there. The bicycle wasn't very big and the doll with the white face looked silly laying there. "What are you thinking boss"? Jake replied, "I think this is some kind of a prank. Someone must be messing with us. I'm going to take that contraption and the doll with us". Dave questioned his partner, "What's attached to the bike"? Jake answered back with a little humor in his voice, "Those are called spoke skins or spokies. They are heavy duty plastic straws and have a slit down the side that can be attached to the spokes by a child. They were popular when I was growing up in the 70's. The more variety of color there was, the better. They made a distinct noise at slower RPM's". "No boss, I'm talking about the baseball card on the back tire". "Oh, that was another common thing. A playing card from a deck of cards, usually the seldomly used Joker, was attached to the frame using a wooden clothes pin. The trailing card flapped against the spokes making a distinct sound". "One more question Jake, what the heck is a clothes pin". "I'll tell you another time". The tired police officer had a hint of irritation in his voice, it was getting toward the end of their shift. "We'll see if anyone tries to claim it, and we'll bust his ass for harassment". Dave grabbed the bike and Jake lifted up the mannequin. They headed back to the squad car. The handlebars on the bicycle had sparkly tassels protruding from the rubber handgrips. It reminded Dave of his new set of bright spinner baits that he was waiting to try out on his next fishing expedition. There was something strange to Jake about the doll. It weighed thirty to forty pounds, much like a live child. Dave ran ahead and opened the trunk. "Jesus Dave, this little girl feels accurately real. There is even a warmth to her. I don't see how this thing propelled down the street so quickly. It had to be going 25 mph"! His partner smiled and made his way to the passenger side of the squad car, still scanning the woods for the tall man in the white gown. Jake removed his Law Enforcement Tactical Knife from the sheath on his belt. He gouged it into the cheek of the doll without much hesitation. He confirmed his haunch. Beneath the plaster face was a red balloon lining the inside of the head. During his elementary days as a kid, he remembered the art teacher, Mrs. McFarland showing the kids how to make a mask for Halloween. They would take these long white powdery strips of cloth, and dip them one at a time into a pail of water. Then they would drape them onto a large, inflated balloon. After completely covering the balloon, it dried overnight, and a hole was cut into the base the next day, big enough so a child could place it over his head. Eyes, nose and a mouth were cut into the orb, and the face was decorated. The body of the doll still felt real as he laid it next to the spare tire. Suddenly, he felt a tug on his gun holster. The doll's small white hand was reaching for his weapon! He brushed the dainty arm away, it didn't seem to have much strength to it. Jake was startled and confused. He could see the back of his partner's head in the front seat, typing away at the computer screen. Maybe an autopsy was in order for this headless creature. He pried the gash of her cheek open a little more and shined his flashlight into the hole. It appeared there was a mass of flesh resembling a brain. It was dry of fluids and had a velvety appearance. Her left knee had a pretty good scrape with a little bit of blood showing. Jake slammed the trunk with many unanswered questions, it had been a long night. Jake climbed into the driver's side. Dave closed out the computer screen and off they went towards the downtown area. "Are we going to file a report on the bike incident boss"? "Hell no, we're going to throw this piece of shit in the evidence locker and wait for a missing person report. Maybe we can catch the perp and charge him with intimidating the police department. I'll have Jan in the autopsy department find the origin of the doll". Dave sensed lots of agitation from his partner. Best not to talk about it this time of night. The new officer had not spent much time in this part of Eagan since joining the department. He had a very eerie feeling about the neighborhood. It was exceptionally quiet compared to the rest of the city. The rich owners never seemed to come out of their houses, traffic was light, and children were scarce. There were no fences between the yards and crime was non-existent in this part of Eagan. Just a few miles away, closer to Interstate 35E, things were a lot different. Over the years, the densely populated areas of Minneapolis and Saint Paul seemed to be spilling into the quieter suburbs. Affordable housing, mostly in the form of dozens of apartments were springing up everywhere in the downtown area. With the low-income situations, mischief and neglect were spreading out from the rental properties. Traffic was increasing, commercial housing was popping up everywhere and criminal activity was on the rise. The quaint culture seemed to be disappearing as viewed by the local elders. The downtown area was the side of the city where Jake and Dave spent most of their time as Eagan Police Officers, not far from Eagan's single police station.

On the way to headquarters, loud scraping noises and low-pitched bumping sounds were coming from the trunk of the car. It was as if someone was in the trunk. The two men looked at each other with surprise. Their faces were pale, and their eyes were widened with curiosity. Next there was a loud moaning noise. A young girl's muffled voice spoke, "You bastards are going to be charged with kidnapping and child abuse you know, you got me in the fucking trunk". The hair stood up on the back of Jake's neck. He accelerated the car down the deserted street. "Dave, why don't we skip the coffee. Call ahead to the station, tell them we would like assistance when we arrive, we'll pull into the lockup transfer garage". Without hesitation, "Sounds good to me boss". When they arrived a few minutes later, they pulled into the secure garage, the steel louvered door quickly closed behind the cruiser. Todd was waiting towards the side. He had transfer assistance duty that night. He was a police officer of brute strength. He stood 6 foot three and weighed in at over 300 pounds. His body was solid muscle, built by the United States Marine Corps. Dave exited the car and turned his key into the trunk, "Looks like we might have a live one in here Todd, …am I glad to see you"! Something was preventing the trunk from opening more than a crack. Todd flashed his light through the gap but couldn't see a thing. He squared off at the center of the trunk facing toward the forward end of the vehicle and curled his large fingers under the metal edge. He lifted with all of his might making a loud grunting noise; the back of the squad car rose off of its suspension with his power lifting maneuver. There was a large popping sound as the latch gave way. "Be careful Todd"! He opened the trunk and the three men peered in. There was a pair of steel roller skates from back in the day. They were the kind that fit over a child's sneakers, snuggly held in under two steel fins, covered in red rubber sheaths. That was all that was there! Todd let out with laughter. "You boys need to call it a night. These double shifts can make you hallucinate". Jake was already going for the office door. He was in no mood for this. The bike was gone and there was no sign of the doll. Dave grabbed the clunky skates and followed suit. He was thankful that they decided on not making up a detailed report. It would have been entered into the station's main computer system, with no chance of deletion. There was no pertinent evidence, no report, therefore no story. Dave refilled his coffee mug in the breakroom. His partner was nowhere to be seen. Looking up at the square silver clock, their shift was finally coming to an end in a few minutes. Tomorrow would be another day.

TWO

THE FIRST WEEK OF HIGH SCHOOL

SCOTT CHESTER FINALLY REACHED HIS freshman year. He only wished that his dad was here to ease some of the anxiety. Not having any older siblings, Scott had no idea what to expect. His father would have prepped him in his unique parenting way, as he always had done in the past with any new obstacle in the boy's life. His dad, Mike Chester was born into a military life. *His* father and grandfathers of at least three generations all served in the U.S. military. Mr. Chester joined the Marines fresh out of high school. His school grades weren't that good, but he couldn't wait to become a responsible adult in the eyes of his family and friends. It was time to become a proud member of the military. He completed most of his training in Twenty-Nine Palms, CA at the age of 18. While awaiting assignment, he dated his high school sweetheart quite steadily. Cheryl was a year younger, finishing up her senior year of high school at the time. She was the captain of the cheerleading squad down at the old Eagan High School, recently turned into a large elementary school. Her body was in perfect shape from her daily aerobic routine. She caught the eyes of many young bucks. The young couple decided to hold off any plans for marriage until a few years down the road. During Cheryl's senior year, Mike was abruptly sent off to Kabul, Afghanistan in late January. Nobody was incredibly happy about the event, it seemed like the most dangerous hot spot in the Middle East conflict. However, Mike proudly fulfilled the mission, to continue to serve and maintain the family tradition. He scored very highly in all his training endeavors. Shooting weapons with perfect precision was his forte. After his first twelve months of deployment, he really felt a passion to get married, especially after not being able to attend his sweetheart's high school graduation. He needed stability at home with the chaos of travelling and most of all, he hated the idea of someone possibly stealing the girl of his dreams while he was away. There wasn't much beauty out in the rest of the world as far as Mike could see. His orders took him to many different countries. Cheryl pondered about attending college like many of her graduating classmates. The constant quiet nudging from her parents also played a part in this natural progression towards the future. However, continuing with education was not a strong desire of hers, even though her academic achievements and grades were astonishing. She was a hard-working attractive young lady who kept to herself. Marriage was also her top priority for now, not more schooling. Mike and Cheryl both wanted to have a large family, they talked about this quite a bit. That year, they decided on a summer wedding in two years. They both decided to take it slow, and to do things the right way. It would solidify a lifelong marriage commitment. Four years of dating would surely purge all the disagreements and differences, so they thought. Mike got called back to the Middle East, the wedding would have to be placed on the back burner as anticipated. Cheryl was so lost without him. She would have nightmares at night, and often see ghostly images of military personnel in the hallway of her parents' house. Her family lived in the quiet town of Waterford, south of the Twin Cities. Sleeping was becoming more difficult as the lonely nights went on. She felt that her boyfriend Mike was the perfect man, and the relationship was becoming stronger and more meaningful, even from a distance. But once again, separation was chipping away at the positive aspects. Over the next year, they kept in constant touch and the long list of planning for the big wedding day had begun. Cheryl had an older sister in North Dakota who gladly accepted the role of Maid of Honor. Dina was the closest person in her life besides Mike. She helped with wedding ideas and offered full support almost daily. Dina always remained single. She became pregnant and had a child nine months after her senior prom, but no one ever knew for sure who the father was. She was seeing more than one guy at the time. Dina had her daughter and raised Sheila with the help of neighbors and friends out West.

The following year, the wedding was getting closer. Cheryl had been shopping around for houses while Mike was away. These missions turned into a hobby for her. Occasionally, her girlfriend Katie would join her along with the real estate agent. The three of them would drive to a half dozen houses in a stint, and tour through each one with open discussions on everything from appliances to landscaping to closet space. Cheryl's desire and wants built up over time as she narrowed her focus. The real estate agent's patience and eagerness faded into the opposite direction as the timeline was stretched. When Mike finally arrived back to the States, it was only a matter of a couple of days before they finalized on a decisive choice of real estate. A four-bedroom, four-bath with 3400 square feet of living space would accommodate their every needs. Mike was elated with his wife's decision, and happily supported her one hundred percent. Anything would be better than living in steel containers out in the Middle East on a dusty steel cot. His future wife managed to do all the leg work in finding a beautiful home for them. He really liked the two-car garage and the large basement. He could see the start of many projects in the future. The manageable sized yard of several acres would also keep him busy on the weekends. Most of it was woods, but the half acre in the front of the house was beautifully landscaped. The property would fester his pride and joy of yardwork for many years to come. There was even a pond deep enough to fish out back. Between both of their sets of parents, the couple had twenty percent to put towards the purchase. The mortgage would be around $1700 per month. With Mike's military earnings and the wealth of the Family's inheritance from both sides, there was no need for Cheryl to work. At a young adult age, she expressed the need of something to keep her busy. Maybe raising children would be the answer in the next realm of their new lives.

The wedding came and went that year during the first week of August. There were 76 attendees, mostly from out of town. It was a beautiful day with the temperature hovering in the low eighties. The festive ceremony reunited the fragmented families to one central place. The reception was held in a park overlooking the Mississippi River. Some of Mike's pilot friends from the MN National Guard, flew three C-130's overhead at an incredibly low altitude. The crowd was pleased and surprised. No one wanted the day to end, but the sun continued its journey to the west. The food was plentiful, the weather was perfect, and all the kids had plenty to do with the well-planned activities. Father Medeiros hung out close to the beer garden, smiling as his alcoholic breath escaped into the summer breeze, chatting with anyone willing to listen. The Family talked about having a reunion every year in the future, maybe taking turns at each other's residences spread throughout the United States. At the end of the day, the family and friends slowly dispersed as the sun sank below the horizon. It had been a perfect wedding with a large acquisition of gifts for their new home, not to mention the huge amount of cash gifted from their wealthy guests.

Shortly thereafter, Cheryl became pregnant. Conception most likely occurred during their honeymoon in Barbados that Fall. The following June, Mike and Cheryl welcomed Scott into the world. He was a beautiful easy-going baby. He slept well and loved to eat most anything set in front of him. Cheryl brought the little guy everywhere, avoiding the temptation of leaving him at some day care facility. The proud mother loved showing him off to everyone she ran into, even strangers at the supermarket. Most of the well-wishers in their inner circle said that Scott had a strong resemblance to his father. Mike spent as much of his free time as possible with his son. Over the next dozen years, he encouraged him with sports, the Scouts and Church. Mike found work as a weapon's instructor out at the MN State Gun Range in Burnsville. He was also one of the top military recruiters for the state, volunteering lots of his spare time for the cause. When he was called for additional tours of leave, he accepted most of the assignments. Cheryl didn't have much say in the matter, but she built up a trust that everything would be okay. The extra money was always nice too. Scott began to take an interest in becoming just like his dad. He liked guns, aviation, and yard work. He even talked of joining the military after his schooling was done. The ROTC was always looking for a constant flow of recruits.

One Saturday afternoon, Mike arranged a little surprise for his son. He contacted a good buddy of his over at the Minnesota National Guard. Brent Lake oversaw the C-130 simulator bays at the Minneapolis Airport. The two of them had a long conversation about his son's desire to be a pilot someday. Mike's buddy Brent came up with a special idea. "How about you and your son swing by next weekend, and we'll play around in one of the sims? The schedule looks light, I think we can get one of them for about ninety minutes". Mike was ecstatic, "That would be great my friend, we have a lot of catching up to do"! "Okay, you're on. Do me a favor though, I need you to bring your son to our main training facility so that we can get a guest ID made up. He'll need this to access the simulator building off 34th Avenue. You'll need your military ID as well. Oh, and can you get a picture of your vehicle and license plate? They've been beefing up the security on the Base, ever since that psycho shot the windows out of the guard shack". "Not a problem. The sim building, is that the big gray building next to the National Guard Museum"? "Yes, that's it. Be sure to have your passport and a driver's license, I will let Matt know you are coming. He will meet you in the lobby of the building to the right of the reception desk. You will receive a call from him later today with the day and time. His name is Matt Cromer. Other than that, I will see you next Saturday at 3PM. Arrive a little early, we'll have some coffee in the briefing room". When Mike hung up the phone, he had to jot down everything that Brent had just discussed with him. *Boy, did that guy like to talk.*

That weekend was a day that they will never forget. Scott was given full access to the sim. He was given instructions from start up at the gate to an instrument landing at a fictitious airport in Afghanistan. He even got a full tour of a real C-130 out on the main ramp. Scott got to see how the ground power unit connected to the airplane to power the entire electric system. Crawling around the avionics bay was like a jungle gym. The ramp was noisy with activity. Large camo-colored planes came and went completing secret missions, probably repetitive training for the most part. There weren't many wars going on anywhere near the State of Minnesota, but the soldiers always had to be ready for the next distant uprising. The active runway was mostly busy with takeoff and landings from the passenger airliners coming from the other side of the airfield.

Inside the air-conditioned building, everything went great for Scott's first sim session, except for the landing. The instructor explained to the boy that this was the toughest part about flying. It takes a lot of schooling before you can become confident and safe. That is why pilots are constantly practicing, followed by rigid check-rides and testing. Overall, Brent said he did very well. Scott's father reminded his son several times throughout the day to listen and pay close attention to Mr. Lake. "Some of his tips may get you out of a bind someday when you finally do become a pilot". The Aircrew Guest ID along with the military lanyard would hang on his son's bedpost for many years to come. Eventually, the boy would convince his parents to buy him a flight simulator game for his bedroom computer. That way he could practice his passion of flying to get a head start towards his career. Mike was honored for what Brent offered to his son that weekend. He enjoyed the day out at the airport as well, seeing the inner workings over on the military side of the MSP Airport. This could be the spark of Scott's career path ahead. Mike would somehow have to return this huge favor to Brent sometime in the future.

During Mike's time away overseas, which were becoming less frequent, Cheryl took care of the house and their son. She continued to be a stay-at-home mom, as Mike made a decent salary with good benefits. The life that they were born into with rich families and few expenses, proudly allowed their savings account to grow over time. Most everything was purchased with cash. The newer, and more established internet helped the couple to stay in constant touch when Mike was away. Cheryl started keeping a box of red wine to the left side of the fridge. She enjoyed the easy access spicket protruding from the bottom of the cardboard box. This magic liquid soothed the loneliness as she would customarily type away on the computer to Mike on many nights. When they were together, she seldom drank. Occasionally after Scott went to bed, the romantic couple would have a few glasses of wine from a fresh bottle, accommodated with a warm plate of hors d'oeuvres in front of the fireplace. Seventies and eighties music created a wonderful ambiance to the room for the two of them. Most of their meals were spent together as a family gathering. Slow cooking and fresh ingredients were a staple in the life of the Chester Family. Scott was becoming well established with school, and the weekends were well planned out, including their weekly ritual of attending Church. The Mass of choice was the 9:15 am on Sunday mornings. Scott didn't particularly care to get up so early on a non-school day, but it was nice to have the rest of the day free to do whatever he wanted. The years rolled by, and the three members of the Chester Family all felt content with the way their lives were going.

It happened just before Scott's 14th birthday. The phone rang in the middle of night, waking both Cheryl and her son. After a minute or so, Cheryl burst out in uncontrollable bawls and howls in a distant part of the house. She dropped the phone as Scott came running down the stairs to the kitchen in his pajamas. His Mom had collapsed on the kitchen floor with her hands over her face. She was in a fetal position up against the island counter, crying and mumbling. Scott shouted, "Mom! Is it Dad?" Cheryl tried to stifle her sobbing, "He's gone!!!! Your father is gone, he was killed last night in Afghanistan! God damn him!" Scott ran to his mother's side as his body gave way in deep emotion, he knelt down next to her. They held each other tightly and cried together for a long time. Scott assured his mom that they still had each other, and they would get through this together. Words did not seem to help; this went on for days. Scott realized over time that he would never see his dad again. No more fishing, spending time at the rifle range and spending hours on end talking about aviation and the military. He looked up to his dad every day. He wondered at that moment if he could carry on without this hero in his life. This cannot be happening; this is the worst nightmare ever. Cheryl was devastated with a mixture of tumultuous hate and compassion. She could not decide who to blame. This consequence of war faded in the minds of family and friends, as Mike was approaching his retirement from the military. For hours on end, Cheryl thought that it must be some sort of mistaken identity of a fallen soldier. Mike never made mistakes when it came to his military duties. The hope was, that this whole event was just a bad nightmare or some kind of mistake.

Over the next few days, the reality hit Cheryl and her son hard, like a brick wall. Neighbors and authorities slowly came to the house, one by one. Some brought gifts, some had kind comforting words, and some just wanted to exchange necessary information. There were not many family members that lived locally, but they would come from afar to visit the grieving household in Eagan.

It was a tough way to spend the summer for Scott, but he had to make the best of it. He was the man of the house now, and he had to speed up his transition into adulthood. His mom seemed to be constantly in deep thought, sort of a ritual haze, and she began to drink alcohol more often. She went from an occasional glass of wine, to sipping the hard stuff from a seldomly used pantry above the refrigerator. The magic of the wine seemed to have faded away. It was no longer strong enough for her needs. Scott accepted his mom's new lifestyle. It seemed to mask all the stress of Dad being gone. He never realized how much she was actually drinking. She managed to hide her habit in a stealthy way behind a deceptive curtain of happiness. On one drunken night, she started to call her son "Scotch". The name kind of stuck on Scott, after all, his favorite treat was a vanilla cone with a butterscotch shell keeping it all together. He loved the new smooth name and was even going to start using it amongst his close friends at school. That would be a nice title as he entered his first year at the high school.

One sober day, his mom took him to the mall. She promised to get some fresh new clothes for the upcoming school year. He hoped that she would spend generous amounts, especially not needing Dad's approval for the spending spree. Scotch had a decent idea of the latest fads at school. He got to see his friends quite a bit over the summer, most of them at summer camp, baseball games and church events. He began to take notice of the way the popular kids dressed. Even at the mall, he observed what the other boys were wearing, often making him jealous of the pretty girls that seemed to always hang out with them. Maybe it was time to find a girlfriend of his own. This was in his thoughts more and more after becoming a teenager. Scott wanted to fit in the best that he could. He wanted a normal life like everybody else.

His mom's biggest surprise gift was a button-down shirt from a high scale department store. The tag said $129 retail. It was loose fitting and had long puffy sleeves. This was almost as expensive as his ten-speed bike that he depended on most every day. With the sleeves rolled up halfway, it was amazingly comfortable. The silky material was out of this world! He got a pair of tan chinos and some nice cordovan leather shoes, along with a matching belt. He decided on wearing this for his first day at the new high school. This would surely get attention from the girls. The anticipation added an extra bounce to his step. The rest of that Saturday, he acquired a few more outfits, socks, and underwear from various stores at the Mall of America. A new pair of sneakers and a denim jacket were also packed neatly into the new Subaru Outback at the end of their shopping spree. They shared lunch together at a nice Italian restaurant. His mom even let him order the buttery lobster ravioli that melted in his mouth every time. Cheryl settled for the eggplant parmesan that was no comparison in Scotch's eyes. The meal was even topped off with a large slice of Chocolate Fudge Cheesecake which they gladly shared after eating so much food from the main course. Conversation was light with his mother, but having her close company, face to face was rather soothing. He couldn't tell the state of mind his mom was in during these days of constant grieving, but she was still very pretty and relaxing to be with. Scotch got a cool haircut at Mr. John's Barber shop (his dad's favorite stylist). His hair lines were cleaned up, feathered on the sides, with a little bit of length to cover up the mole on the back of his neck. It was a great day Scotch recalled, except for the constant trips in and out of the fitting rooms. The stiff new clothes against his sunburned skin, and the stabbing price tag that always showed up in a sensitive area (such as under the arm pit) added to the grueling task of trying things on. That was getting old, but Mom had to give the final approval, she was paying for it all. Over and over, he undressed and dressed and walked back out into the public to find his mom. The comments were always similar. "That looks nice, turn around. Stand up straight, you're slouching. How does it feel. Slide your belt buckle to the center. I like that color on you". Even the sound of the wooden louvered door opening and closing with the irritating click of the knob added to the misery. He just wanted to get it over with and go back home.

Scotch and his best friend Ricky were going to be in the same homeroom together the following week. They would see old faces from elementary school, as a lot of the students were split up into four separate Junior High Schools for the 7th and 8th grade. It was possible for two neighbors to attend the same elementary school, but different Junior Highs. This had to do with the school district boundaries and bussing requirements. Scotch felt that the next four years were going to be full of big changes. He outgrew his nerdiness, and he was feeling stronger and looked better in his newly developing adolescent body. Ricky was still not up to par, but he was a good support friend who boosted Scotch's confidence. They did everything together. Scotch believed he even looked more impressive to others next to his lanky friend Ricky.

His Mom came into his bedroom at 6:30 am that Monday
morning. He was awakened by the shades being rolled up, and the
smell of bacon and coffee following her into the room. It was very
difficult to get up, especially after the summer hibernation from
school. His alarm that he carefully programmed the night before,
didn't even get a chance to work. Scotch thought about making a
deal with himself to lay there for ten more minutes after his mom
left, making sure the alarm function was still in good working
order for the rest of the week. The anticipation of his first day of
high school put an end to the thought. He shifted the alarm clock
off and sprung out of bed. A stretch and a yawn brought him to
life. His morning breath smelt and tasted terrible. The morning
sky was barely showing much light at this early hour. His mom
offered to give him a ride to school on his first day. He agreed
and headed off to the shower down the hallway. As he shuffled
towards the bathroom, Scotch looked forward to his new daily
task of lathering up with shaving cream, and carefully gliding
the razor across his face. It was not as awkward as last Spring,
a little more natural feel to it now. The peach fuzz would soon
turn into stubble, at least this is what he hoped for. The warm
shower transitioned him from the lazy weekend to the task ahead.
The breakfast was nice as it brought back memories from the
past, when Scotch and his parents would spend most every meal
at the same table. Besides Dad not being there, something was
different. Mom had not joined him at the table like she always did.
She read the newspaper while standing up at the island counter.
Her reading glasses smudged with fingerprints hid the beauty
of her facial features, the lenses foggy in appearance from the
side. Her hair was snarled together into a haphazard bun on top
of her head. The small television announced the daily headlines
in the background, not much good came from there. He really
missed the conversations they once shared. He kind of felt this
during their school shopping excursion the week before. The

normal conversations were absent. Scotch knew his mom was still grieving with the loss of Dad. He was also becoming a young adult. Not much guidance was needed like when he was younger. He quickly finished his cheese omelet loaded with mushrooms and onions while closely watching the clock hung over the kitchen sink. "Mom! Where is my shirt"? "It's hanging in the living room by the ironing board, you're welcome". "Thanks Mom". Scotch found it hanging with several other items on the chintzy clothes rack that Cheryl liked to use for her ironing chores. One of the items was a red silky nightie that Dad had bought Cheryl for Valentine's Day earlier in the year. She never wore it. There it was freshly washed and ironed along with some flowery dresses. Scotch wondered if his mom would ever date another man. Why else would she wear those things? There was a side of him that hoped not. His shirt gleamed in the morning sun. The weave of his dress shirt had a shiny striped pattern throughout it. The buttons looked like white ivory, mounted on ornate brass bases. It looked better than before! No creases or tags, mom really took the best of care to get his outfit ready for school. He could not wait to put it on. His chinos with the matching belt and shoes were going to be a hit! He wondered if he would have more than one girlfriend this year - maybe even some secret relationships all at the same time. What a year this could be! Not all his classmates were interested in dating. The reasons were many, including lack of spare time, having parents against the idea or just plain lack of social skills and/or decent looks. Scotch was a quick learner though; he watched the older boys closely. Things were going to be much different at the new school for him.

Homeroom attendance was slated for 7:45 am. The school was about a 10-minute ride from the house. As he was slipping on his shoes, his mother was collecting all the dishes and putting them in the dishwasher. Cheryl had just come in from the back porch, where she liked to have a morning cigarette with her coffee. Listening to the birds and observing the creatures of the forest were a bonus to starting the day anew. The kitchen reeked like an ashtray as she wobbled the top rack into the dishwasher and closed the door with her foot. She came back into his life again, "Did you brush your teeth mister"? He replied "No, I'm good". She barked back, "Don't get smart with me, we don't need any extra dentist bills around here. Now get up there and make it quick! I'll back the car out". Scotch finished up quickly in the bathroom. He smiled into the mirror and bushed his hair one more time, forgetting to turn off the light. He grabbed his mostly empty book bag, hopped down the stairs, jumping over the last two. After the ten-point dismount he ran through the kitchen and headed for the garage.

Scotch climbed into the Subaru idling in the driveway, welcomed by the droning radio host on Mom's favorite AM station. She clicked the button on the overhead visor to close the garage door. Traffic and weather report were to follow immediately after a short commercial break. They would hear the same repetitive loop a couple of times before they arrived at the school. As they pulled into the new High School, Scotch could see many familiar faces. There were many that he did not recognize too. The school was enormous and dozens of freshly cleaned yellow-orange school buses slithered their way up to the front of the school like a long, fragmented snake. The newer busses had tinted windows and the exterior decorated with the new style of halogen lights. The standard features were always the same. Scotch's Uncle Charlie explained to the boy many years ago that the three black stripes known as the "rub rails" on the side even had a purpose. The bottom one was the floor level of the bus, the middle one is where the student is seated, and the top being the top of the seat. That way when the bus is involved in a rollover or deposited into the nearest body of water, the first responders have some guidance with opening up the can of kids as quick as possible. The rub rails also served as reinforcement to add to the integrity of the bus for further protection during collisions. Scotch reminded himself that he never had the opportunity to commute on these long student transporters because he lived close to all the schools that he attended. He was only able to ride on a school bus in the event of a field trip, which added to the excitement of the annual daytime outing. Were there any field trips left in his lifetime now that he was entering high school? The sidewalks were lined with students. Everyone looked anxious and jubilant, many dressed in new clothes. The kids exited the busses in a methodic way, and the empty vehicles made way for the next group of busses. As Scotch climbed out of the Subaru, he turned to tell his mom through the opened passenger side window that he would be walking home from school with Ricky. Cheryl nodded with a sideways smile and a tear in her eye. She paused for a moment and put the window up, slowly pulling away from the curb. Scotch was off to his freshman year at the big high school. Cheryl was instantly hit with memories of her first days of school. Her worrisome mother always seemed to smother her with love on those special occasions. The mornings were not complete without pictures of her and her sister in their new school clothes. Dina and she would stand by the maple tree in the front yard while their mother captured the moment with the black and silver Polaroid. Her father always missed the occasion, leaving for work before sunrise each day while the rest of the family slept until it was time to get up. Those days seemed so far away now. She cracked open the window and lit the Lucky Strike between her lips. Maybe it was better to be an adult now, free to do whatever she pleased. She tossed her lighter into the car's cup holder and flicked the first ash out the driver's side window. In no time, the car's interior visibility began to diminish. It was time for a little bit of adult shopping as she comprised a list in her head. She opened the window a little more and sped out of the schoolgrounds as the traffic cop hurried the flow of cars. As the obnoxious referee whistle faded from behind, the cigarette smoke got sucked out of the car window.

The students conversed in small groups, loud and chatty. The conversations were filled with excitement and anticipation of their new teachers at a new school with new classmates! The landscaping around the school was well manicured by the summer groundskeepers. The brightly colored American Flag wavered proudly above the front entrance to the school. A loud metal bell rang from the top peak of the building. The students slowly made their way through the double entryway at the front of the school. They walked the corridors looking for the homeroom number that was mailed to them over the summer. This event was followed by the sound of closing doors, and chairs being pushed in and out across the linoleum floors above and below at the multi-level monstrosity of a school. Teacher's voices were heard trying to contain the chaos. The hallways were soon empty. Scotch made his way to the back of his home room after hanging his fleece in the closet. He saw his best friend Ricky seated next to a shy girl named Lucy. She was blushing in front of his best friend as the two of them exchanged small talk. Was she embarrassed for being seen next to Ricky, or was there some kind of romantic relationship forming there? Scotch sat down in an empty chair beside them. After attendance was taken, Mr. Roberts assigned everyone to their permanent seats and issued padlocks for their assigned lockers. The locks were a shiny chrome, with a black dial that rotated on the face. The teacher was a serious man in his early sixties who was happily approaching retirement. Fortunately, Ricky's new seat assignment was right behind Scotch. This would assure important conversation daily between the two best friends. Ten minutes later, the overhead bell rang again. The kids had five minutes to get to their next class after attaching the padlock to the assigned locker. Scotch was amazed at what happened next.

Stephanie's locker was right next to his. She was the prettiest girl in the whole entire high school. He followed her progress over the last few years as she blossomed into a beautiful flower. She was dressed in tight white pants highlighting her curved buttocks with a beige, loose-fitting sweater. Her blonde curly hair was flowing halfway down her back. The bright color of her shiny heels tied in nicely with her thick leather belt. The air around her smelt like mints, fruity candy, and perfume. Her teeth were as white as could be and her lipstick shined her smile to perfection. Without missing a beat, Scotch said "Hi Stephanie, you look very nice today". She smiled slightly "Thanks, you don't look so shabby yourself". Scotch smiled back, possibly blushing as well. That is all they had time for. Scott was glad that his mother made him brush his teeth. Having egg breath might have changed everything that morning. Scotch hardly noticed Mitch was standing a short distance away. He was the star athlete in several after school intramural sports. His body was large and sturdy. Growing up on his family's dairy farm seemed to have formed his athletic body, although there were rumors of steroid use as well. Mitch hung out with the tough guys and the pretty girls. Mitch did not like the losers at Eagan High.

The hallways filled rapidly with a constant flow of students in the short time between classes. They emptied just as quickly, ending with the sounds of slamming lockers. As the day went on, the flow patterns seemed to get a little more organized. There was lots of chatter as students became accustomed to one another. Social circles were beginning to take shape for the school year ahead. As the kids got older, it seemed they were more decisive of who they wanted to hang out with, and who to avoid.

Scotch's classes were good so far, the teachers seemed fair and not much homework was assigned on the first day. His third class was Algebra. His friend Ricky was in that one. Before class started, everyone was having private conversations with one another. He mentioned to his best friend the desire to maybe date Stephanie sometime this year. Ricky replied, "I wouldn't do that if I was you, she is still dating Damon Wheeler". Damon was a bully they knew from elementary school. Scotch had not seen him in a couple of years, but he recalled all the taunting incidents from years ago. "I thought he moved to another state"? Ricky replied, "He did, but now he's back again, his parents got divorced". Scotch got a lump in his throat. The eavesdropper Mitch had already told Damon about Scotch talking to his girl that morning in a provocative way.

When Scott was filing through the crowded hallway towards the Study Hall, he met up with Damon. The boy had grown four inches taller and put on about fifty pounds. He was bigger than Mitch! His clothes were tattered, and his muscular body showed through everywhere that it could. He was coming right towards Scotch. His large stubby red nose was distorted with acne, new and old blemishes. "Stay away from Steph you punk, or there's going be trouble". Scotch snapped back without thinking "She's not yours, dude"! What he meant was that she was not married to Damon, and therefore Stephanie could decide *who* was to be in her life. It did not translate that way to the angry monster. Damon got right in his face, "How about we meet after lunch out on the north field and take care of this the proper way, pretty boy". The ugly nose was close to his face and Damon's breath smelled like garlic and sweat. Scotch said "Whatever!" and walked away. His father always taught him to stand up to bullies. If they see that you are not afraid, you will have a much better chance of survival.

At lunch, the cafeteria had hundreds of students. Everything was so much larger than his two previous schools. The classrooms were a lot bigger. The high school included a multi-use gymnasium, an outdoor as well as an indoor swimming pool, and a skating rink in a separate building out behind the school. The Fine Arts Building and the Planetarium complimented the large campus. Ricky and a couple of other boys joined Scotch at one of the round tables. They talked about their new classes, teachers, and girls. After lunch, they went outside to hang out for the final fifteen minutes of the lunch period. Scotch seemed socially distant to his friends that day. He kept gazing over at the north field. It was a large open grassy expanse, frequented by the athletes of the school. Scotch had no plans for sports in his future. He had no reason to be on that field. When lunch period was over and the bell rang, they broke off to head to their next class. At that point, Scotch realized that Damon never showed up after his threat this morning. Just as he thought, it was probably all for show. The north field remained empty except for a dozen brightly colored orange rubber cones with black bases. They were either left out from an earlier gym class or put into place for some after school activity.

The rest of the afternoon went slowly. Scotch kept watching the clock. The bell finally rang, and it was time to go home. He was to meet up with Ricky over by the gymnasium for the walk home. He placed some of the new textbooks in his locker, the ones from classes with no homework assignments. No sense in carrying extra weight around. The new numbers to his padlock were starting to become familiar to him. Pretty soon, he could ditch the code typed up by Mr. Roberts that he kept tucked away in his wallet. He slammed the steel locker door closed, turned the dial on the padlock a few times and made his way towards the exit. He could hear the heavy steel door close behind him as he followed the paved foot path. As he was coming around the back side of the building, he noticed about ten faces looking right at him on the north field. Damon was in the middle of it all. His snubby nose stood out. Scotch had the urge to run, but he knew that he had to tough this one out. He would use some fighting skills if he had to that his father taught him from the military. First though, he would attempt to talk his way out of any confrontation. As he was approaching Damon, some words were exchanged. Damon was going for the first push. As Scotch stood firmly to retain his balance, he tripped over an obstacle behind him. It was Brian Leaky, crouched down on all fours behind him. Scotch never saw him get into his stealthy position. He toppled back, and the crowd began to laugh and clap. The newly acquired contents of his book bag from the first day of school spilled into the parking lot. Scotch forgot to zipper the top of the bag closed. Damon immediately reached down and grabbed Scotch by the shirt in the clenches of his fists. He lifted him to his feet with a ripping noise and two of the ivory buttons popped off his shirt. Damon's long grubby fingernails pierced the white fabric, leaving scratch marks in Scotch's soft skin. Hygiene was not one of Damon's strong points. The bully was strong and quick with very decisive moves. This was followed by an upper cut to the nose. Scotch saw a sharp light while experiencing a pain to the front of his face, and the strong urge to sneeze. Large spatters of blood and spit arched above his head. Damon released his shirt, and Scotch fell to the ground. Sandy Wesson came forth from the crowd and gave Scotch a swift kick to the crotch after another kid stood on the boy's fingers pinning him to the ground. He never saw the painful kick coming. Sandy was the girl bully of the school. Her face was freckled with acne, and she was a little on the heavy side. No chance of her missing out on the action. At that point, he curled into a fetal position as he trembled in pain and confusion. He had a strong urge to vomit. Someone else kicked sand into his eyes. He couldn't see. *Was that Stephanie standing over him a second ago?* He was a mess, with no one to help him off the ground. He felt burning scrapes on his left cheek, embedded with small gravel and sand. He began to sob; he was totally defeated and couldn't hold it back any longer. Damon injected the final words to the ordeal, "Didn't put up much of a fight you little wimp"! The crowd drifted away with laughter as they disappeared around the corner. Eventually, Scotch got to his feet, gathered his books, and limped towards the gym. During the commotion, he thought Damon had dropped something. He scooped up what looked like a biker's wallet at the edge of the parking lot, partially hidden by the tall grass. It was a worn leather wallet with a six-inch length of broken chrome chain dangling from it, and an evil looking skull stitched on one side. He slipped it into his torn chinos. One of his shiny leather shoes was scuffed deeply across the front. Shoe polish was not going to fix that one. His "walk home escort" was approaching in the distance. Ricky saw his friend limping towards him with his white shirt ripped open and blood all down the front of him. Scotch's facial expression was twisted, and his hair was a mess. He ran to support his friend's mangled body. "What happened man"? Scotch managed to fight back the tears and exclaimed, "Damon and his asshole friends ganged up on me out behind the school". Ricky said, "I told you to stay away from her, didn't I"? "Fuck you Ricky, thanks for your help"! Ricky jumped back at first, he didn't know what to say. He tried to brush some dirt off the back of Scotch's shirt, most of it was there to stay. The two boys walked off towards home, with very few words exchanged. Scotch knew that the pain would go away eventually, but the embarrassment in front of his classmates was unbearable, especially the girls. Everybody would probably hear about this over the next few days. The schoolyard brawl would become more falsified and embarrassing as the rumors spread. What the fuck happened; this was not a good way to start off his new year at the high school. His favorite clothes were ruined as well as his reputation. His new adult complexion would probably be bumped back a notch with permanent scars. When Scotch got home that afternoon, he headed right upstairs to his room. His mom must have been out running her daily errands. The weekday afternoons always ended with acquiring some non-healthy food and a bottle of booze for the evening ahead in front of the TV.

As Scotch undressed and slid into sweatpants and a sweatshirt, he could not believe how many scrapes and bruises covered his body as he looked in the mirror. He washed up with a hot washcloth. *Why did his mom have to always choose white towels?* As he gathered his balled-up clothes on the floor, he decided to hide them deep in his closet. His eyes were filled with tears. That was his favorite outfit, and he only got to wear it once. His mom spent quite a bit of money at the mall, she was not going to be happy with him. He would have to figure this out later. For now, he just wanted to climb under the covers and die. He suddenly remembered the wallet! Scotch jumped up and went to grab the beige chinos hidden at the bottom of his hope chest. He retrieved the wallet and returned the tattered clothes to their hiding place in the closet. The boy brought the wallet over to the desk light. It was dirty and grimy; he was almost scared to look inside. It had the smell of wet musty leather. There was a $10 bill and several one-dollar bills. There was a student ID that read Damon Wheeler with an ugly picture of the jerk, he had a crooked smirk on his face underneath his ugly nose. There was one more item behind the bills. It was a folded-up piece of a magazine page, in the shape of a rectangle with some writing on the face of it. It was labelled "1 gram". Scotch's best guess from what he learned in health class last year, was that this was $100 worth of cocaine. This was the typical packaging. Revenge to Damon! He brought it over to the trash barrel by the nightstand. What would be the best way to get rid of Damon's hooch? His nervous fingers slowly unwrapped it, and he spread it out next to his alarm clock. He thought for a moment, then took the ID and spread the mysterious powder into long thin lines. He took the ten-dollar bill and rolled it into a tight tube, like he had seen on a TV crime show. He inhaled the powder through his nose while slowly moving the tube down each white line until they disappeared. He wanted to sneeze at first, and there was a terrible taste of aspirin at the back of his throat. Then it all went away. A euphoria like never before was filling his thoughts. He was drifting into a faraway place of silence. Suddenly, the silence was interrupted. He could hear his mom pulling up the driveway in the Subaru. As the heavy garage door opened, it vibrated the walls. The sound of her engine got louder as it echoed in the garage, followed by the vibration again, while the garage door slid closed along its tracks. The engine went quiet, and the car door opened, then closed. He quickly snorted the last of the evidence, wrapped everything in a dirty sock, except for the cash, and hid it in his book bag. He would dump the stash back at the schoolyard where he found it, keeping the cash for his troubles. He jumped onto his bed and opened a book just as his mother closed the entryway door into the kitchen. He pulled the top sheet up to eyes and propped one of his books up on his chest. He could hear his mother unloading the groceries from the brown paper grocery bags. Both the refrigerator door and the kitchen cabinets opened and closed several times. After climbing the creaky stairs his mom peeked in shortly thereafter. "How was your first day honey? Don't tell me you already have homework." Scotch replied, "No, school was alright, I have some awesome teachers and it was nice to see a lot of friends that I haven't seen in a while. Not much homework, just getting a jumpstart for tomorrow". "Alright, I'm going to watch the Laws and the Orders, there is some chicken patties in the freezer. I'll drive you to school again tomorrow, I have some morning errands to run after that". "Thanks Mom, see you in the morning". She didn't even comment on his face. He cleaned up the best he could, but there were still cuts, bruises and new areas of swelling. Hmmm. A minute later, he felt odd. All the pain left his body, and his quiet room started to cool down. Something strange was happening. He placed his headset over his ears, turned on some Pink Floyd, and floated off to another world. The drug was beginning to fill his nervous system, jetting along in the flow of his blood. He felt strong with the urge to laugh out loud. The loudest explosion that he would ever hear would happen later that night, as he fell fast asleep for now.

THREE

MYSTERIOUS VISITORS

SCOTCH'S FIRST WEEK AT SCHOOL finally came to an end. He was feeling better, and no one seemed to give him any flack about the schoolyard incident. There was one run-in with Damon again though. It all happened when Scotch was headed to the boy's room with a pass from the teacher. After he entered, Damon had followed in behind him, probably without the required hallway permit. It was still morning, and Damon had a habit of coming into school late. He didn't seem to mind the constant visit to the housemaster's office to explain himself. 'After school detention' gave him an opportunity for an afternoon nap or a chance to draw cool stuff on his book covers. Scotch felt Damon's presence after seeing a glimpse of him in the mirror. Scotch went about his business. Damon pulled up to the urinal beside Scotch. Looking straight ahead and talking out the side of his mouth, "Did you take my wallet the other day, you little punk"? Scotch barked back, "Why would I do that, fuck you"! "You better realize who you're dealing with, I might just decide to mess you up again". Damon thought about the wimp's wrong answer. Someone with the sound of dress shoes was walking down the hallway towards the men's room at a very rhythmic pace. Damon zipped up, smiled in the mirror, and exited back out into the hall with the heavy door closing behind him. Scotch was nervous and uncomfortable as he finished up taking a leak. He walked over to the sink and looked up into the mirror as he washed up. *What just happened? The asshole does not seem so physical without his friends around, otherwise he would've kicked my ass again. He could've even urinated on my new sneaker.* His dad's advice seemed to work about standing up to bullies. Damon is still going to be a problem though. What did Scotch do to deserve this? Maybe he needed to start lifting weights, bulk up a bit. This would give him a better chance for his future. It was times like this that he wished Ricky wasn't so nerdy. Maybe he could convince his friend to join him at a gym, with a dedicated membership. They could work out every other day during the week, maybe even once on the weekends.

That Friday after school, Ricky invited Scotch over to his backyard swimming pool. Ricky's Dad was going to make burgers on the grill when he got home from work. After checking in at home with his mom, he emptied his book bag and refilled it with a bathing suit, sandals, sunglasses, comb, and a towel. He opened the garage door, jumped on his bicycle, and glided down his driveway towards Ricky's house. This would probably be one of the last times to enjoy an afternoon swim this season, the Minnesota air was starting to get cooler. On the way out of the neighborhood, he was met by Mr. and Mrs. Bonfilio. They always liked to chat for a bit. Bob was a retired postmaster who lived each of his retirement days for golf and Agnes was a retired schoolteacher who loved her afternoon walks. She taught U.S. History at one of the local colleges for 37 years! They never walked too quickly. Scotch thought to himself that they don't walk to stay in shape. The elderly couple was only exercising the brain to convince it that it can still get the body from point A to

B, one step at a time. They were always so bubbly and talkative; it would be rude to pass by without stopping for a chat. After an unimportant conversation about nothing, he continued on to his friend's house. After laying his bike down on Ricky's front lawn, he knocked at the front door. Ricky's sister Gillian answered the door. She was in a tight one-piece yellow bathing suit brushing her long hair with her free hand. "Hey Scotch, come on in. Ricky's out back by the pool. You can get changed in the bathroom; I'll tell him you're here". "Thanks Gillian, are you going to join us for a swim"? "I'm thinking about it, I have to get my stuff ready for dance class first". "Well alright, see you out back in a few". Scotch liked Ricky's older sister. She had a lot of spunk in her, and her body wasn't half bad, especially in that yellow bathing suit. It was going to be a good afternoon. He exited the bathroom and headed for the back sliding door by the kitchen. Ricky's Mom was just headed out with a plate of freshly baked chocolate chip cookies. "Hi Scott, it's good to see you. Are you going to stay for supper tonight"? "Yes mam, but my mom says I have to be home around six". "Perfect, Fred will arrive around 4:30, I'll have him start the grill when he gets here". Closing the screen slider behind him, Scotch saw Ricky lying on a lounge chair by the pool. Scotch spread out his towel on the chair next to him. "Well, are you going to tan or swim"? The lounge boy yelled, "Last one in is a rotten egg!!!" Ricky jumped up and dove into the pool after a quick sprint. Scotch replied, "No fair, that was pre-meditated warfare". He jumped in after his friend. Gillian appeared from the house, her body shiny with suntan lotion, and she smelled like a tropical coconut. She entered the pool using the stairs in a very lady-like way. Shortly thereafter, the three of them started a Marco Polo game. For the rest of the afternoon Gillian and Scotch flirted with each other, Ricky was the third wheel. The diving board and slide got full utilization and the cookies went quickly. Ricky's Mom interrupted the fun. "Everyone out of the pool. Gillian, dry off. It's time for dance class. We have to leave in the next fifteen minutes. Ricky, your father will be here shortly, help him get the grill ready. I'll be back in an hour". Gillian and her mom left in a hurry; the boys jumped back into the pool. Scotch floated around on his favorite inner tube. Shortly thereafter, Ricky did a cannonball on the edge of the float after it drifted close to the diving board. Scotch resurfaced, "Hey you jerk, you busted my back"! "Sorry dude, I just meant to splash you, ya know, to clean you up a little bit". Scotch yelled back "Ya right, payback's a bitch". The cool water felt good on Scotch's body, soaking the scrapes and bruises that he got at the beginning of the week. After a while longer, the boys started getting cold and wrinkly, especially at the fingertips. After they climbed out and began to dry off, Ricky's Dad pulled up in the Bronco. He waved from the driveway, dressed in an uncomfortable looking business suit. "Hey boys, hope you're hungry! I'm going to get changed into comfy clothes. Ricky, can you preheat the grill, I'll be out in a few". "Sure Dad, Mom and Gillian are at her dance lesson, they'll be here shortly".

After Ricky's dad prepared the food, they all joined together around the long wooden picnic table. Ricky's mom brought out a salad using fresh vegetables from the garden. Scotch sat next to Gillian. Occasionally they would accidentally touch their bare legs against one another. Nobody seemed to notice. The afternoon quickly ended. After a quaint backyard picnic, it was time for Scotch to head home. He thanked Ricky's parents for supper and flashed one last smile at Gillian. Maybe they would get hooked up someday thought Scotch to himself.

The long-awaited weekend was here. That Saturday, Scotch awoke on his own while the house was still quiet. His mother usually vacuumed with her trustworthy Oreck and did the laundry, on Saturdays and Sundays. Looked like she was getting a late start this morning. He still had his ruined clothes hidden for now in the closet. Eventually he would have them washed and repaired at the local dry cleaner before his mother noticed anything missing. The Korean lady that worked there seemed to be a wizard with clothing that needed attention. Maybe she could even mend his scuffed up shoe. On his agenda over the next two days was yardwork, homework and maybe some fishing. He always had a list of things to do in his mind. Sometimes his mother would design most of it, with the simple persuasion of an allowance. His fooling around with the flight simulator often chipped away at his allocated time, making it a tight schedule. Ricky didn't come over as often as he did during the summer now that school started. Summers were always the best time of the year!

The yard work came first. This was a chore that Scotch enjoyed, and his mom gave him $20 each week for his efforts. It was probably the most exercise he was getting, other than riding his bike to and from school. His dad left them with a large array of tools that was collected over the years. Most of them had their own hanging place on one of the walls in the garage. Once in a great while, he would have to borrow something from Mrs. Ricker next door. Today involved some trimming around the garden areas with the electric weed whacker, mowing the grass for one of the final times of the season and a little bit of light raking. The oak leaves would start to fall over the next few weeks, welcoming the harsh Minnesotan winter ahead. The raking would become most of the labor for the next couple of weeks, with the snow shovels anxiously waiting next in line. Most of the leaves had lost their green appearance, with vivid colors slowly taking over, especially with the sugar maples that dotted the Eagan neighborhood. His favorite purple hooded MN Vikings sweatshirt would be needed to make the cool temperature tolerable, at least to start the job. The first barrel of debris was hauled down back to the compost pile. With the steepness of the hill and the roughness of the path, due to constant erosion from heavy rains, it was not always an easy task. Tripping on the rugged path was an expected consequence. Today though, a full barrel wasn't all that heavy. The air had been dry for a couple of weeks now. Some of the tree roots from the giant oaks overhead exposed themselves across some of the trails. There were several paths branching off into the woods. Over the years, Scotch would occasionally rake them clean to define the walkways to the pond and the compost pile. Green vegetation would grow on the sides that were not walked on. Minute flowers would occasionally poke through the green undergrowth. The pond was about 30 yards across, filled with mostly turtles, frogs, and crappies. His dad had stocked the pond with bass over the years, but few of them remained. His father told him the Sunfish, or the Blue Gills as Minnesotans call them, would eat all the Bass eggs. When Scotch caught the smaller 'sunnies', he would toss them far up into the field grass for the night-time predators. This was his way of helping the reproduction of Largemouth Bass. The ancient pond was spring fed and around 8 feet deep in the middle. Occasionally a snapper turtle or some mischievous black racer snake would find their way into the quiet oasis. As Scotch was returning up the hill to the back of the house, he remembered the quake from the other night. He put the empty gray Rubber-Made barrel down and wandered over to the taped off area. He lifted the yellow crime tape and slipped underneath. As he approached the crevice, he could not believe the size of it. He looked down into it, but the narrow hole ended in darkness, not much to see. It was worthy of taking a closer look when all of his chores were completed, and he still had some daylight left. Back to the yardwork, it would be getting dark soon, and Mom was making a special batch of chili for them tonight. She was a great cook when she put her mind towards it. This was happening less and less though. Drinking in front of the TV seemed more important, with an occasional smoke break out on the back stoop.

After a final run to the compost pile, Scotch had an idea. He grabbed his old flashlight from the garage that his father had given him. This souvenir flashlight was the size of a pack of gum and held one AA battery. It said Walt Disney on the side, and when you pressed the button on the top, a little door flipped open on one end and the light came on. A little beaded chain hung from one end, to clip onto a belt loop. The chain was surely not the caliber of the chain that Damon had on his lost wallet. Mike got it for him at a gift shop during one of his military training seminars down in Florida many years ago. He promised his son that when the boy got a little older, he would take him to Disney World. That day never came.

Scotch returned to the crevice just as the sun was starting to set. He donned on his hooded sweatshirt that he hung on a small tree by the garage. The cool night air was beginning to settle in. He thought he could hear some voices coming from underground. It sounded like they were speaking in a foreign dialect, much like what he heard the night of the explosion! Also, there was circus music playing faintly in the background, deep within the crevice. Trumpets, trombones, and tubas were playing a joyous melody with an occasional pair of symbols clashing together, very distant though. He grabbed the old wooden ladder leaning up against the woodpile and carried it over to the opening. It was a tight fit, but it would get him to the bottom of the deepest part, where it looked like it flattened out into a dark cave. Upon reaching the last rung, his dim light shone ahead into a dark walkway. The thought occurred to him to come back in tomorrow's daylight when it would be safer. Then he justified that it would be dark in a cave no matter what time of day it was. He walked for about twenty feet into the darkness at the base of the crevice and rounded a bend to the right. There was a light ahead that was getting brighter as he walked further, producing much more of a glow than his childish flashlight. He clicked it off. This more powerful glow was a bright yellow light, not very natural looking. The air was getting cooler and moist with a musty dirt smell. The sounds of the birds and the crickets out in the woods were fading behind him as he walked. The distinct pitter patter of his footsteps was becoming muffled. Suddenly, he found himself standing in a large open part of the cave. A dozen heads turned toward him; their bodies draped in darker attire. Hoods covered the shadows of their tanned faces with their eyes glowing as dim yellow lights. The unexpected vision caused him to back up a few steps. There was a table in the middle of the room with these men seated around it. The yellow light seemed to be coming from the base of the walls and at the top of the walls. The source could not be seen, it was almost as if the walls had background lighting. The shadowy figures had no facial features, and they were accompanied by a leader in a long white robe. He was very tall and looked Middle Eastern. Scotch estimated his height to be well over 7 foot as he stood up. His orange face was dignified and stern sporting a black mustache and beard. They were finely trimmed. His nose was long and straight. The whites of his eyes were large with dark brown pupils in the middle. The face had an expression of a profoundly serious man that meant business. He had a white covering over his head that may have been attached to the robe. A black roped ring kept it all contained. The mumbling of the foreign language immediately stopped amongst the small group. All eyes were on Scotch. He felt the urge to run back to the ladder, but his legs felt paralyzed. This looked like a dangerous meeting that no one from above ground was supposed to know about. The tall man approached him after coming out from behind the long table. His name was Khalif. He was speaking to Scotch without saying anything. It was as if they were reading each other's minds through thought. After some observation of each other, ideas and thoughts began to flow into each other's minds. This was taking a lot of energy; Scotch was starting to feel worn and drowsy. He was not interested in the rest of the group for now, only Khalif. He felt the stranger was from far away, sent here to protect Scotch and his mom. Had they arrived from deep within the Earth? How were they going to protect them, and what from? After a few minutes which seemed a lot longer, Scotch felt as if Khalif had formally dismissed him. Before doing so, he handed over a silver chalice with some sort of red liquid in it. Scotch needed both hands to accept the offering, it was quite heavy. The boy planned on taking a small sip so as not to be rude. When the taste of it touched his tongue, the experience was out of this world. The cold liquid tasted like every favorite fruit of his and it felt thinner than water as it flowed across his tongue. Scotch tipped the heavy goblet from his mouth, and Khalif grabbed it back. He could have easily drunk the whole thing, but it was not an option. Suddenly the thoughts and conversation between him and Khalif were more detailed and natural. Discreetness from the outside world was the top priority, Scotch was to tell no one of his encounter. He sensed a ton of danger in this strange place, although he felt there was a trust between them. It was too dangerous to return to this cave anytime soon. He slowly turned and walked towards the hallway. Just around the corner, there was

a huge underground lake! The water was crystal clear with a sandy
bottom. There was a bluish light illuminating the water. Gigantic
fish filled the water. Their outlining colors were amazing. The
ceiling was a deep blue, illuminated with stars. Scotch could not
identify what species the fish were, but the fluorescent-colored
edges of the fish were aglow like neon lights. Normally, Scott was
used to seeing fish at a standstill if there was no current. Here,
there were twelve or so, circling like sharks in the shallow water.
Khalif yelled at him from within, "The exit out of here is the
other way! Go in peace and you have sworn to me your secrecy
to the people up above"! Startled by the loud volume of the voice,
Scotch made his way to the other dark hallway that he came in
from. His eyes were adapted to the darkness at this point. As the
air started to change, something caught his eye to the left of the
tunnel. He was at a distance now, away from the men in the room.
In front of him was an old wooden trunk with two leather straps
holding it together. He must have walked right by it on the way
in! A latch of some sort was on the front of it. Beside the trunk
was a shiny object laying in the dust. Scotch reached down and
scoffed up a coin quickly. As he continued towards the ladder, he
turned and looked back. The circus music started playing again.
It almost sounded as if it was coming from an old AM transistor
radio. The acoustics were not that clear. He felt like a group of
people, or some kind of an energy was following him back up to
the surface. There was only darkness with nobody in sight. He
climbed the ladder and pulled the old rickety thing out of the
hole. The sun had set. He clicked his flashlight back on. He
carried the ladder back over to the woodpile. After tripping over
a protruding rock, he realized that his flashlight was inadequate
for this adventurous sort of thing. Over by the woodpile was the
firepit that had not been used in quite some time. A lot had
changed since his father perished in Afghanistan. Scotch removed
the coin from his pocket to get a closer look. Someone was

watching him. It was Mrs. Ricker on the back of her porch. Her eyes were emitting a red glow in the evening twilight, even though she was 60 yards away. There was a distinct crackling noise coming from her lips. Something was not right, Scotch's hair stood up on the back of his neck. His attention shifted back to the coin in his palm. The circular piece had a man's profile on one side and a shield topped with a king's crown on the other. It appeared gold in color and had a date etched on one side with words written in a language that he could not understand. The date was 1787. Scotch's dad often told him about hidden treasure in the area. British troops were stationed in this region at Fort Saint Anthony during the Revolutionary War, and the Indians were getting forced to move West. Somewhere in Eagan, the Indians supposedly buried gold that went missing from the barracks. The plan may have been to retrieve the loot at a future date. *No way, this cannot be related.* He tightened the coin into his closed fist and looked over at the neighbor's house. She was gone! No sign of her. What was the old lady looking at anyways? Scotch never believed most of his dad's stories as the boy got older. *Could this gold treasure one be true*? He had an idea. He would try to find the worth of the coin, maybe at the library. This would be kept secret for now, nobody else had to know. Where would his research begin? He knew nothing about coins. Then he had an idea that would solve his problem. This called for a trip to the Old Coin Shop near the school, next to Paramount Rugs. The coin had to be worth something.

That night at the dinner table, Scotch had lots of questions for his mother. Unfortunately, she was already halfway in the bag. She was bubbly and cheerful, but her words were slurred. They were both finishing up their second helping of chili. "Mom, what do you know about Mrs. Ricker next door"? She took a deep breath and replied, "Well, Annelle Ricker was one of the first in the neighborhood. She is supposedly from Indian descent; Dakota Indians that is. Her great grandparents worked in the onion fields that existed before this neighborhood was ever built. She told me the Indians were not accepted as normal people and would hide in the shadows, so the early settlers had to be vigilant of the forests. This was their land before the white man came and stole it from the Native People. The fighting went on for centuries, there is still murmurs of it today. Annelle was married to a Mr. John Ricker up to about the time you were born. We do not know what he died from, but he left Mrs. Ricker all on her own. They had an adopted daughter that would be a couple of years older than you, but I believe she was sent to a mental hospital upstate. Mrs. Ricker has been genuinely nice to us over the years, letting us borrow stuff and keeping an eye on things when we are not home. She keeps to herself; I think her husband was in the army or something". Scotch said, "Oh, that explains the reason for that big green army vehicle in the driveway that never moves". She laughed a little bit, "Yeah, that piece of shit has not run its engine in years. It is quite an eye sore for all of us neighbors". "The *other* neighbors that we never see?", questioned Scotch. As Cheryl poured herself another fresh glass of bourbon and began to clear the table, "Be thankful for the peace and quiet around here, some people outside of this neighborhood have to live on the other side of the tracks, where evil and chaos creeps into their life from every direction". The quietness was nice, especially down by the pond. Her son didn't like or trust *that* lady next door, but it was nice to finally know a little more about her.

After the dinner table was cleaned up, Scotch and his mom talked about a few other things. He agreed to start taking his bike to school more often, even walking on occasion. This would save gas and help with the bills. Being dropped off by your mother wasn't cool anyways, Scotch assured himself of this. He finished drying the dishes that his mother had just washed and then put them in the cupboards, as his mother had one last smoke for the night beneath the porchlight in the backyard. He hoped that his mom would hear mysterious sounds, maybe circus music or a glimpse of the witch next door staring over at the moths fluttering in the light. No such luck. Cheryl retired to the living room anxious to watch some TV while she sipped some more bourbon. Scotch went upstairs to his room to complete his daily homework.

Cheryl didn't have to push him much; Scotch always completed everything he started, and he had a strong desire to learn new things. Mike was a good father to him; he gave his son a strong foundation in his earlier years. His Mom hoped that her son would find a stable career after graduation, side stepping the military tradition of Mike's family. It was too much risk and wars never turned out well. Scotch was all that she had now, and she would like to have grandchildren someday. The homework was almost finished, and Scotch decided to work on flying the Boeing 747. Out of all the aircraft profiles on his computer simulator, the 747 was his favorite. It was larger and faster than the other planes. He could start the simulator session anywhere in the world and the chosen airport would have every detail. He could get fancy to break up the boredom by programming malfunctions to the aircraft, basically sabotaging himself. On a few occasions, the mismanaged situations would end with a red screen after everything came to a screeching halt. Simulated death wasn't so bad he thought. He could always reboot the simulator and start over fresh.

Scotch shut down his computer and folded back the sheets on his bed. He decided to finish the rest of his homework tomorrow. It felt a lot cooler tonight, so he lowered his window with only an inch to spare. He checked that his alarm clock wasn't set to go off and thought about encouraging his mother to attend church with him tomorrow. The thought subsided quickly. It would never be the same without Dad. He headed into the bathroom to brush his teeth and comb his hair. He was thinking about the strangers in the cave. He almost had the urge to bring them out some food and blankets. *What did they have to eat? Maybe the fish. How long were they going to stay in the dark and cold cave? What happens if members from the Eagan Parks and Recreation Department come to fill in the dangerous hole over the next few days?* He did not have the answers. He finished up in the bathroom and decided to visit the fridge downstairs. Might as well check on his mother while he was at it. The living room had the lamp turned down very dim, the TV was off, and the chair was empty. Maybe she was in the basement putzing around. As he opened the fridge, the red fruit punch caught his eye. It wouldn't be as good as the stuff that he had down in the cave, but it made him smile of the memory. He took three big gulps and returned the bottle back next to Mom's wine box. As he turned to go upstairs, he noticed the back porch light on. He must have forgot to turn it off earlier. Looking out the window of the back door, he could see two moths fluttering around the bright light. Someone was out in the woods. The dark silhouette was coming up the path towards him with a bright flashlight. Because of the light, he could not make out a face. Could it be officers Jake and Dave, checking up on things? The light was within twenty feet of him now, he was starting to feel scared. The beam of the flashlight clicked off, and he could see a face, it was his mother. He flung the door open. "Mom! What are you doing out there? You scared me"! In a slurred voice, "Oh, I was just bringing some scraps down to the compost pile. I don't know if we're making new composted soil or just attracting the critters". Scotch was amazed at her calmness, "Mom, aren't you scared of the dark woods"? She laughed a little bit, "There is nothing to be afraid of out there, I only bring the light with me so that I don't trip on any of those dam tree roots". Scotch didn't agree with "nothing to be afraid of". There were lots of things that were strange out there, he was beginning to hear and see many things. They both returned into the house, and the lights went off one by one. The moths returned to the darkness of the woods, or perhaps they went out to investigate the beams of light emitting from the overhead streetlights in the front of the house.

The weekend was over, it went by quick for the boy. He looked forward to the second week of school, if only he wasn't nervous about Damon and some of the other bullies. He wanted his start at the new high school to be better. It will be a long four years if things don't change. He decided to be on the lookout for cooler people to hang out with. A membership at the gym was on the agenda as well, with or without Ricky. He would stay low profile and try to avoid the classmates that teased him. A girlfriend would be nice to have. That would be a way to find new circles of friends. Scotch grabbed for his headset. He slipped the padded muffs over his ears. He popped in one of his preferred CD's and laid back on his bed. He reached up for the lamp and switched the light off. In a very short time, he drifted off to sleep.

FOUR

STRANGE HAPPENINGS

I T WAS AN UNEVENTFUL MONDAY at the high school. There was only one pop quiz, and not much homework. The meatloaf served up in the cafeteria was one of his favorite meals. After school, he headed over to the coin shop, parking his bike out in front of the tiny store. Scotch pulled open the heavy glass door and slipped inside. A loud sharp ding sounded as he entered the shop, probably for security purposes. The walls were lined with glass cases supported by steel frames and filled with individual coins. The plate glass windows in the front of the store had steel grates on the outside. An old man in his late seventies stood at the far end. He had funny looking glasses on with a microscope apparatus to one side of his left lens. The store was bright with overhead fluorescent bulbs shining down on the long cases, a couple of them were emitting a buzzing sound from their dusty ballasts. "How can I help you today young man"? "I have this coin I wanted to show you, wondering if it is worth anything", replied Scotch. "I found it in the woods behind my house, it's kind of dirty". He placed the coin onto the glass counter and watched the old man look it over like he owned it. His hands were suited with white cotton gloves and his sports coat had the aroma of moth balls. He slowly started to speak, "Evveerry coin is worth something, it's all about rarity and condition, that's why.... hmmm...hang on for a second. I'll have to get one of my Spanish reference manuals in the back. Do you mind if I clean it up a little bit in the back? It won't hurt the value any". "Sure, that would be great". He trusted the old man right away. The guy had to have been around coins for decades. If he didn't know his stuff, he would surely not be in business today. Scotch looked through some of the cases as he waited for the old man to return. There were many coins that were various metallic colors and all different sizes. The rare pieces were individually sealed in between two panes of white cardboard with a clear plastic protector holding the coin. There was information handwritten below the circle window. Some were worth many dollars compared to the original face value. There was a 1932 silver quarter for $4.95, a 1932S quarter worth $37, a 1914 Buffalo Nickel worth $15 and a 1915 Liberty Head dime worth $40. A larger coin in the adjoining case, close to the size of his coin was a 1964 Kennedy Half Dollar worth $5. The next case over had much older coins. Some of them resembled his own find in the 'Spanish coin section'. He quickly found one dated 1780, it was silver and had a face on one side. It had the words "Carolus III D.G. on the perimeter of the coin. It had a price of $25. Wow, that would be quite a return he thought. After what seemed forever, the old man returned with a smile on his face. "Surprise, surprise, surprise.... how much do you want for this one son, I'd love to have it"? Scotch excitedly approached the counter. The old man went on. "This is an exceedingly rare "Escudo" coin. This coinage circulated from the time of the Spanish Empire in the Americas. Nobody knows how many are left out there, but it is indeed quite rare. We are looking at 3.38 grams of .875 gold". Scotch was perplexed, "How much is it worth". He explained that in today's money, it would be worth $150 (in reality, $210, but the young lad didn't need to know that). "I can give you cash right now kid"! Scotch thought for a moment, "No thanks, I'm going to hold onto it for now. You have some neat stuff in here, someday when I'm rich, I'll be back". "Yeah, sure thing, I will still be here. Make sure that door closes all the way on your way out, thanks for stopping in".

As Scotch left the shop to head home, he could not believe the worth of this coin. The shop owner cleaned it up very nicely too, at no cost. *What about that large trunk back in the cave? What was in there? Was it filled with more of these?* In the meantime, Scotch remembered about his first history report coming due in a few days. Maybe he could present the class with some interesting research on this coin, he could tie it in with the local history. This might get him an "A" in one of his toughest classes! Stephanie was in his class as well. Maybe they could work on this together. He was already forgetting about the pact to himself – nobody needed to know about this coin or anything to do with the mysterious cave. The other students would figure it out though when he started showing up to school in a limousine. Just like every other American, it was fun to dream about being rich someday.

That afternoon, Scotch decided to head down to the pond to do some fishing, after running out of time on the weekend. He needed some time to think about past events and the absence of his father. This would be one of the first things that his dad would do after returning from overseas. The two of them would not harvest many fish, but it was quiet and peaceful back there and they could catch up together on life. Once it got dark, an armful of logs burning in the firepit would not be out of the question. Sometimes his father would run up to the refrigerator in the garage and get a handful of thick beef hotdogs. The two of them would each whittle a stick to a sharp two-pronged fork and roast the wieners over the fire. They tasted the best that way. He leaned his bike up against the wall in the garage and headed into the house. Looks like mom was home early from her errands. The car was parked on her side of the garage. As he approached the kitchen, he saw a note on the counter. The house was quiet and dark. SCOTCH, BILLY PICKED ME UP TO GO TO DINNER AND THE MOVIES, WE'LL BE HOME LATE. THERE'S CHILI IN THE FRIDGE, I'LL TALK TO YOU TOMORROW. Billy Preston was a neighbor that Scotch never liked. His mother went on a couple of dates already with him. He was a short skinny man, five years older than mom. He wore the same clothes all the time, and he reeked of cigarettes and beer. Dad never liked him either. Billy would often sit in his backyard Adirondack Chair and pick off animals that were in the woods behind our house, a bottomless can of beer beside him. It did not matter what species they were, he just liked killing things with various weapons. Preston never talked to the boy or his dad, and there was always screaming coming from the depths of the neighboring house. Dad came up with the assessment that the drunk man beat his own wife because she was not sexually attracted to the slob anymore. She eventually moved out. Dad thought he might have seen Billy looking into the windows of their own house, probably scoping out Mom in her pajamas, but he was never able to prove it.

As Scotch made his way on down the path, something made a noise in the trees above. When he looked up into the treetops, he could not believe what he was seeing. There was a humongous buffalo standing in the "y" of one of the oak trees, fifty feet above the ground. It was surely alive; his tail was twitching back and forth. This was a full-grown mammoth like he had seen at the Minnesota Zoo. He remembered that at a young age, he crouched down and reached into the pen to pat a buffalo's tail. It spooked the buffalo, and he kicked the fence throwing the boy backwards. He was always afraid of large animals after that. The thick brown fur and large horns were vivid and mesmerizing. He continued towards the pond to see the animal at a better angle. He looked up again, and it was gone. *How the hell did that beast get up there, and where did it go?* He is positive he saw this; he could even hear the animal making a quiet snorting noise. Something struck him suddenly. Was Damon's white powder that he snorted causing him to see illusions? Did he have a concussion from the schoolyard beating? What about the red drink that Khalif gave him? He did not have the answers. At this point, he really needed to get his fishing line out into the water and go into deep thought before the first hungry fish went for his worm. Scotch could also watch for signs of the buffalo to return from a safe distance. He opened the clear plastic lid of the blue and orange Maxwell Coffee can, containing the worms that he collected over the weekend. He snatched up a fat lively one. He worked the shiny hook through the neck and fed it through the body towards the tail. The rest of the tail was worked through the barb a couple of times. Uncle Billy taught him a lot back in the day and would always say – "A human must be smarter than the fish. If you let too much of the night crawler hang off the end, the fish will grab and pull without getting near the barb of the hook. You're just feeding them at that point. Then someone like me will come along and catch the fish that you fattened up"! Scotch rinsed his hands with a few splashes in the pond and made the cast. Perfect one, the bobber was right under the branch of the distant birch tree on the far side. Over the years, lots of hardware was lost in those trees, but not today. Scotch was getting really good at his casts. The larger bass seemed to like the shadier areas. Scotch plopped himself down on the grassy embankment and began to ponder. *Should he be telling an adult about these strange occurrences in the backyard. Would they even believe him?* The risk of losing that treasure chest before he found out what was inside, would really be a bummer. Something else bothered him that had nothing to do with the woods. *Why was he not accepted by all the other students at school? After all, he wasn't a nerd, he dressed well and came from a good solid family background. Was it a carryover from when he was younger? Was it the crowd that he hung out with (the ones that were going to be successful in life)?* He would probably never learn the truth. Some people were just bullies, and the popular kids sided by those types so that in turn, they themselves wouldn't be bullied. Scotch decided that he would avoid confrontation, do the best that he could with education, support his mother and live life as normal as possible. Being a pilot with the Armed Forces was not out of the question. Dad always said that a military path in life would be the cheapest way of getting the required flight training and later, Scotch could transition into the airlines. As he looked across the pond, he admired the water's surface, smooth as glass. An occasional bug or small fish would break the surface. Scotch would watch for a larger fish or a turtle to retrieve it quickly before it disappeared. The birds chirped happily high above in the tree branches. Occasionally, a pair of gray squirrels would chase each other throughout the woods. In the distance, through the tree branches, Scotch could see his neighbor Billy, throwing a stick to a large black dog. In his other hand, the loser of a man clutched a can of his everyday staple. Scotch never wanted to be like his neighbor, he wanted to be just like his own Dad. *Where was his mother, she was nowhere in sight? The note said that she was with Billy. Aaah, maybe it was a different Billy.* He envisioned a tall slender man in a suit who had lots of money and travelled the world. This fictitious man was now ready to settle down and enjoy the good life with a beautiful woman like Mom. But Scotch still had a bad feeling about the more likely picture. He lay back against the embankment to the pond. It fit the contour of his spine perfectly and it was covered with soft green grass that would slowly turn brown with the approaching winter ahead. This would be the perfect opportunity for a short nap. No more ~~than a minute later, his~~

bobber disappeared. He felt a firm wiggle of his pole. As he stood up, something was startled and made a large splash to his left, the opposite side of where his line was pointing. He looked over expecting to see an otter, beaver or muskrat wanting to go after his fish. Something big made that noise. Whatever it was, it was under the surface of the water and headed straight for him at a horrific pace. A triangle of water that was 3 feet long, trailed behind the hidden object. Suddenly it turned and Scotch could see it beneath the clear surface; the boy's eyes just about popped out of his head. It looked like the head of the largest snapper turtle ever. Various markings were on the scaly skin and the eyes were large and yellow. Struggling to see its shell behind the head, Scotch realized it was a snake! If he lost his footing on the slippery embankment and fell in, he would be a goner! It had to be 20 feet long with a head that was bigger than his waist! It was thrusting its body in an S pattern, moving quite effortlessly and streamlined as well. The monster veered to the left as if distracted by something. Scotch relaxed his stance and tried to get a better look. Then the head of the creature broke the surface of the water and lunged back towards Scotch! It did an instant reversal as it came within five feet. Its body splashed down hard and was now headed to the far side of the pond, the head slowly submerging below the surface and the wake disappearing into the black water. The surrounding water filled in the crevice of the wake. *How quick would it move once it was on land*? If it was like any other species of snake, Scotch knew the answer. He dropped his pole and ran for the house. Meanwhile, he startled a rabbit from the compost pile. After it ran a short distance, it paused and stood sideways in the path leading up to the house…. but it had a small human head on it. It turned its neck to face Scotch and smiled at him. It had a small man's face with rosy cheeks. The head was bald with two hairy rabbit ears attached. The face reminded him of the old man down at the coin shop. The rabbit then turned up the path and darted at the speed of light, disappearing into the brush. Suddenly, an overhead branch snapped. As he gazed toward the treetops, he saw the buffalo's large brown body falling towards the ground. It brushed several branches on the way down. The large mass hit the ground with a powerful thud. It immediately thrashed around in the leaves to find its footing and stood its massive body back upright. It was staring right at Scotch with its big black glassy eyes as if it was the boy's fault for the mishap. From fifty yards away, it tucked its large head and began to charge in the direction of Scotch. The brown wooly fur on its back was covered with dust and leaves. Scotch continued running up the empty pathway to the house at a sprinter's pace, probably faster than the rabbit. He arrived at the back entrance of the house all out of breath, opened the screen door, entered, and locked the back door behind him. The mammoth beast leaned its body and changed the direction of its charge to the side of the house. Snot and dust slung outward in the opposite direction, The sound of galloping hooves through the wall of the garage faded out almost instantly. He removed his muddy shoes, placed them in the corner of the garage and raced for the entryway into the house. The cold cement floor on his sweaty feet made him move at an awkward pace. He locked that door as well and ran to one of the windows in the front of the house. There was no sign of the buffalo or any of the neighbors to witness the bizarre event. The boy trudged on up to his room. The note from his mother still rested on the island counter. He looked out his bedroom window across the woods. Nothing looked abnormal, but it was also getting dark pretty quick making features hard to pick out. He wondered what kind of fish was on his rod anyways. *What was that rabbit all about? How did the large buffalo get up into the tree, and then survive a fall from so far up? Where did the massive snake come from?* Anacondas are a very large species, but they're not from around here! He would maybe check out the woods tomorrow after school. Hopefully, he didn't lose his dad's expensive rod and reel. It would be very costly to replace. The thought occurred to him to get the bright flashlight that Mom had in the junk drawer, but he knew the forest was becoming more dangerous with each passing day. Further investigation would have to wait until daylight.

After he put on his slippers, he went to the kitchen. There was no mail on the island counter, only the letter. He decided to go out to the mailbox to retrieve the daily mail for his mother. The last part of the house to see daylight was always out front. It faced to the west where the sun set every night. As he was walking down the driveway, he saw that the Bonfilio's were passing by on their daily walk. "Hello neighbors"! Scotch yelled out. Their faces stared straight ahead with a look of disgust. "Hello?" They continued to walk. *Were they in shock from seeing a buffalo, did somebody hurt them or take something away from them or did they just go deaf?* Scotch jogged up to the back of them. They both turned. Something was wrong with their faces. It was as if they had featureless masks on. The only thing recognizable were their glasses and their attire. Mister had his plaid shirt on and his straw hat, Mrs. had her yellow jacket and her walking cane. The two of them suddenly turned in the opposite direction and began to run. They had to be pushing early eighties and they both had a hard enough time walking. Now they were sprinting like twenty-year old Olympians. Scotch couldn't believe his eyes. In no time, they disappeared between two houses and ran off into the shadows of the woods. Scotch didn't have a chance of catching them. In all honesty, he didn't want to catch them. He went back to the mailbox and retrieved the mail. There wasn't much that day. He headed back into the house and shut the garage door. Mom had her own key if she decided to come home tonight.

FIVE

NEXT DAY AT SCHOOL

SCOTCH WOKE UP TO HIS alarm clock at 6:40 am. He was very hungry as he made his way down the stairs. After everything that went on yesterday out back, last night's supper was skipped. The kitchen was cold and dark. He peeked into the living room to locate Mom. Her empty chair had the quilt folded up on the back of it. She never returned from the date with Billy.... *how could this be*? He decided that she was a grown adult going through life changes on her own without Dad. Scotch would sit down after school later today and discuss this with her; just the two of them, adult to adult. He toasted a couple of slices of bread, not even sure if they were stale or still hanging on, slabbed them with butter, and added some strawberry jam. A glass of orange juice would complete this gourmet breakfast. After opening the refrigerator door, next to his OJ was a six pack of Heineken beers with two bottles missing. *Mom did not drink beer, this was odd.* He finished his breakfast, got ready quickly and headed off to school on his bicycle. He checked to see that his gold coin was still in his pocket. The coin went everywhere with him. It felt as if it had special powers, seemed to give him good luck as well. He enjoyed the bike ride to school. It gave his hair a chance to dry naturally, and the fresh fall breeze put him at peace. Sometimes he would switch things up and take the longer route by the St. Paul airport. He loved to see the aircraft out on the ramp, especially the larger ones. Aviation activities seem to have slowed down with the recreational side of flying. The summer was over and fuel prices climbed quite a bit over the last six months. Aviation gas was always more expensive than what automobiles pay at the pump. His father once explained that the refineries must go through special processes to obtain higher octanes required for aircraft engines.

After homeroom, he needed to get to his locker to get an English book for second period. Last night's assignment was to prepare for a short quiz today. He would have to study during first period Economics for a swift recovery. At the locker, Stephanie was busy switching out books. "Steph, how you doing"? Not bad, what is going on with you? Without hesitation, "Check out this gold coin I found". Her eyes lit up. She asked to hold it. "How much is this thing worth"? He was anticipating that very question. He explained that it was assessed at $150. "I think I know where there is a whole trunk full of these. It is sitting in a cave that I discovered near my house. It is kind of risky to take a closer look though". Her wheels began to turn. "I visited my cousin this past summer in North Carolina, we went into a couple of caves. They were dark and musty. We even saw a bunch of bats! I know how dangerous they can be". Scotch could not believe he was having a real conversation with this beauty. "I'm planning on doing some research on this and applying it to my history project. What do you think"? She replied with guilt, "I haven't even started my project yet, that's one heck of a course. How about we get together this Friday night at your house and work on it together? I am good at writing; you seem good with creative ideas". With some concern, "What about your boyfriend Damon"? "Oh, he won't care, we 're just friends now, he is interested in another chick. He treats me kind of crappy anyways". "Let's do it then, can you meet me at 5:00 on Friday? Wait, do you know where I live?" "Yuh silly, don't you remember me selling cookies for the Girl Scouts 3 years ago? You came to the door in your pajamas. You were such a nerd back then". Scotch embarrassingly replied, "I don't remember, but I bet the cookies were good". "Alright, see you on Friday, gotta go"! As she turned and strolled off, her walk was like that of a super model. Her faded jeans looked like they had been painted on. Her body travelled out of the locker area with just the right amount of wiggle and stride. Curvy muscles and cool confidence were the drive behind that machine. *Man, has she turned into something wonderful!*

Scotch could not wait to tell Ricky about this one. He just scored with a date.... with the prettiest girl on earth! He will have to come up with an idea for *her* project. In the meantime, more research would have to be done at the library on this strange coin. A head full of intelligence is a great characteristic for a single man to have. Scotch remembered his best friend's warning to stay away from her. What a bind he was in, messing with Damon's woman. The good seemed to outweigh the bad though.

Stephanie wasted no time. She met Damon out in the parking lot after school. He had his mother's Buick Skylark. Dating an upper classman did have advantages. She told him all about the expensive coin and the possibility of a whole trunkful in Scotch's backyard. A windfall of money would help Damon to purchase that little sports car he was saving up for. He surely was not saving that much money so far. She often wondered where all his money went. Steph exclaimed, "Baby, I think I can get a hold of this money, I have a plan"! "You're one crazy broad, what are you thinking"? "Well, on Friday, I'll meet up with Scotch at his fire pit out in the woods. After a little bit of time, you can meet up with us. While you are kicking his ass, I'll go check out this

SIX

THE NEIGHBOR NEXT DOOR

SCOTCH MADE HIS WAY THROUGH the overgrown hedge between the two houses. It had spaces every few feet, entangled in some sort of an ivy. Thorny branches grabbed at his clothing and skin from every angle. He protected his eyes by holding up his arm. The branches scraped his forearm leaving thin bloody slashes. The front door of the house would make the most sense to pay a visit to Mrs. Ricker. He paused at the old 2 ½ ton Army truck, resting partially in the bushes on the edge of the property. He had never paid much attention to it in the past. The heavy steel bumper reached out quite a distance from the rest of truck, draped with chains and a heavy reel of steel cable just forward of the engine grate. A blanket of orange pine needles surrounded the vehicle from the feathery pine trees overhead. The windows were foggy and covered with pine pitch and bird turd. The green camo color was holding up decently, chipped only in a few places. In front of the driver's door, it had large letters "CCKW", and a large white star painted on the center of the door. His dad told him that it was a GMC from the forties, a true workhorse in the second World War. It had a strong smell of oil and canvas. The back of the truck was enclosed with a canvas top and sides, giving the vehicle the appearance of carrying a large loaf of green bread. It was over 9 feet tall. The tires that its heavy body stood on were almost as tall as tractor tires. They were faded almost to grey from the sun and there were chips of rubber missing in some spots. Over the years, they somehow retained their inflation. Towards the back, it smelled strongly of some dead animal carcass and urine. That kept Scotch from looking any further. He swayed to the right of the behemoth vehicle and headed for the doorbell at the front of the house. It had been several years since he saw Annelle up close. The yard was unkept, except for small amounts of seasonal planting. Most of the plants never made it into the ground, remaining in their original pots from the store with the descriptive labels fading with time. The pavement on the driveway was barely visible, cluttered with dirt and dead debris from the trees above. The yard was over foliated with trees and bushes. Vines hung down from the larger oaks resembling Tarzan ropes, stripped of all foliage. The thick forest gave the house more privacy and cooler temperatures in the summer, but it was as if the woods was winning a battle, leaving the weathered house in a sort of disarray.

The front stoop was as welcoming as the rest of the yard. After one ring of the doorbell, he waited a bit and then knocked lightly. He could hear some shuffling feet approaching the door, getting louder with every step. A low toned raspy voice yelled "Go around to the back porch! What the hell's the matter with you! [The steps shuffled away from the door, getting quieter with each step]. "Stupid kid"! He was not sure if this was a good idea to even follow this woman's instructions. She sounded as if she had gone insane. Her raspy voice sounded mean and pissed off. Scotch felt committed, so he made his way to the back of the house. The flagstone walkway was blackened and crooked. The back door was already opened, and there was an exterior storm door that remained closed. He could see Mrs. Ricker standing there in a dirty housecoat. As he approached her, he noticed her face was old and wrinkled. Her silver hair was snarled and matted. She had bloodshot eyes, with a crooked purplish nose. Looked like it had been broken several times in the past. The woman never faced him directly which seemed disrespectful, or maybe she was hiding something. Her eyes gazed out into the woods as if she were blind. Only her profile was visible through the dusty glass. "Hello Mrs. Ricker, I'm Scott from next door". Her muffled voice came through the glass, "I know who the hell you are, what do you want"? Her raised voice huffed condensation on the dirty glass door. "I was wondering if I could borrow the aluminum ladder from you, I'm cleaning out the gutters in the front of our house". "You're just like your old man, always borrowing stuff. Where the hell has he been lately anyways, is he overseas fighting in the desert sands"? "No mam my dad was killed in combat last Spring. It's just me and Mom now". Her voice softened somewhat, and she pushed the storm door open a crack, enough to protrude her head from the house within. "Jesus Christ, I didn't know. I am sorry to hear that young man, I liked your father very much". "Well, he was the pinnacle of our family, we miss him dearly. Someday I'm going to join the military and continue his legacy". The woman spoke more clearly now, "I don't know if that's such a good idea, stay home and take care of your mother. Having family around is a big part of life, trust me, I know". Scotch was trying to avoid looking directly at her gruesome face. It was only a couple of feet away. He felt a feather touch his left eyeball and blinked, still looking down. As he looked toward her direction, he felt it again. He just caught a glimpse of a large snake tongue coming from the woman's lips. It was forked, had a sandy texture like a cat's tongue and smelled of rotten fish. She had just touched his eye with it. "What was that for!!!!?", exclaimed Scotch. Almost at a whisper, she replied "I was just taking a little sample of your soul….". Her soft voice went away. The strong cackling with overpowering authority returned. "The ladder is under the deck wrapped in a blanket. Bring it back clean or I will have your hide! And don't fall off the damn thing"! "I won't mam, I'll wrap it back up, and put it under your porch when I'm done with it". "Make sure it's clean and knock at my door when you return it, THE BACK DOOR! And stay the hell away from John's truck, I don't like people nosing around where they're not supposed to"! [Little did Scotch know, Mr. Ricker's mutilated body has laid in the back of that truck for years. His body was gutted with a hunting knife and cut into sections with a hatchet. The old hag wrapped the carcass and its appendages in industrial plastic several times, sealed it with duct tape and deposited it in a rubber-lined canvas bag that John had laying around from the Army. It was closed tightly with a couple of stainless-steel hose clamps. A decade ago, Mr. Ricker was getting to be a pain in her ass. Now, the miserable bastard was no longer a problem.]

Scotch thought of her as an odd human being. She seemed very frustrated about everything. He guessed that loneliness could drive a person crazy. He would take good care of her ladder so as not to upset her. She returned into the house and closed the door. As he started to unwrap the canvas, the package was filled with spider cocoons, webs, and dried leaves; what a mess. As he felt something crawling up his arm, his vision shifted in that direction. It was a large black spider with yellow markings. The ladder was dropped, his free hand brushed it to the ground. He went to step on the thing, but it disappeared back under the porch. He checked to make sure she was not watching through the faded curtains, then unwrapped the rest of it quickly. He balled up the paint blotched, moldy canvas and shoved it back beneath her porch. He carried the long silver ladder through the hedges and over to his house. As he brushed it through the bushes, and bumped it against some trees, he thought that any loose bugs would fall off. He laid it down on its edge and leaned it up against the back of the house. The yellow nylon rope was a tangled mess with the ends wrapped in loose electrical tape. Scotch knew how to fix that. His Dad showed him skills on how to braid, tie proper knots and how to burn nylon rope with a butane lighter to prevent the ends from fraying.

Scotch entered back into his house in case Mrs. Ricker was watching. He lied about the reason for borrowing the ladder, but the real truth was top secret stuff. He made a quick ham sandwich and poured a glass of milk. Suddenly the phone rang. As Scotch reached for the phone on the first ring, he could hear his mom snoring from the other room with the TV turned up kind of loud, no sense in waking her. It was Aunt Dina from Minot, North Dakota. He hadn't talked to his aunt in quite some time. He normally got all her life updates from his mom. He learned that his older cousin Sheila was fascinated with horror stories since her teenager years. After graduating with a high school diploma, she decided on becoming a mortician. Most funeral homes require prior experience, good personal skills to comfort the grieving families, and a bachelor's degree. She was lacking in some of these areas but found a business in Idaho that would hire her. Hopefully it would just be temporary. Aunt Dina didn't like her only child to live so far away. The aunt lived quite a distance away from her sister Cheryl, but she had her own life out West with lots of friends. The young mother worked for a beekeeper at a large honey manufacturing plant. Dina was the head CPA, in charge of keeping the books clean and organized from day to day in case the IRS paid a visit.

He talked quietly with his aunt for quite some time, told her all about Mom's current situation. Things were not good here in Eagan for her. "Scott, I'll talk to her tomorrow before she runs her errands. I think she should hop on a bus and come out to visit for a few days. Sounds like she just needs a change of pace." "Sounds good Aunt Dina! Don't tell her what I told you". "I won't, she'll tell me everything on her own, in time. Will you be alright by yourself for a few days"? "Yes, I will be fine. I just want things to be the way they were when Dad was around. I worry about her". He hung the phone up and headed down back into the woods with the ladder by his side. Changing the grip several times definitely helped going down the uneven path. He slid the 20-foot extension ladder into the crevice. No need to extend it out, 10 feet was all he needed. The young lad backed away into the woods to take a leak. He had been holding it for quite some time. You could barely see the top of the ladder from a few feet away because of the dirt berm built up on the north side. Suddenly, something caught his eye. A large hairy twig was moving rapidly from below the rim of the hole, shifting side to side. Another twig appeared, the exact same size. Then two glass marbles appeared between the twigs. It was a giant-sized spider scaling the ladder up out of the hole! The black eyes rotated from its bases in unison staring right at Scotch. It was very fidgety but moving swiftly for its size. It had to be 15 inches across! Scotch hated spiders, even small ones. He jumped back and decided to go down into the cave another time, maybe tomorrow. It was starting to get dark, and he left his flashlight up in the garage, anyways. Then he noticed some red fire ants between him and the hole. As he looked down to find the source of them, he realized there were hundreds of them. As he shifted his gaze towards his feet, they were all around him, moving rapidly in every direction. They were even behind him. Suddenly, he felt them crawling up his pant legs. He turned towards the path, for a rapid escape up to the house. The ladder could stay where it was for the night, maybe the creepy spider would be eaten alive by the ants. He ran as fast as he could while brushing his legs. Some of the ants had made their way into his shirt. They were starting to bite his skin. It was as if hundreds of hot pins were penetrating his body. A couple of them came out of his hair and were crawling on his cheeks. He brushed away and smacked his own body while keeping a consistent running pace. After reaching the back patio, he slipped his shirt off over his head and started to unbuckle his belt. The bites were stinging, burning, and itching all at the same time. Prickly legs and antennae were moving all over his body! He looked down at the ground. There were no ants on his white T-shirt that he just slipped over his head. He kicked it around with his sneaker, checked his pants. There had to at least be some dead ones. After looking closely at the ground, there was no sign of any ants. Did he just imagine the whole thing? His pants were clean also. He got redressed after double checking for insects. The puzzle was starting to take shape. Whatever these strange sightings were, the buffalo, the rabbit, the snake; it had to be the work of the tall man, Khalif. Scotch was not sure of the reasons behind the creations, but he could only assume that the team of servants down below could take on different forms, no matter how abstract. They seemed to transform to hide their true identities and carry out different sorts of missions. None of these creatures have harmed him in any way, other than scaring the crap out of him. *Should he visit with Khalif, the leader, to confirm this?* There was no answer that came to mind. Maybe he should let things be, and just concentrate on the retrieval of the trunk for now.

SEVEN

BLOODY THURSDAY

SCOTCH RODE HIS BIKE TO school on Thursday morning. It was a beautiful sunny day. He had a toasted bagel wrapped in a paper towel in his backpack, some stray peanut butter smeared on the zipper of the book bag. He stayed up late Wednesday night messing with his Boeing 747 simulator computer game. Someday he will fly one of these, it was always in the back of his mind. The military C5 would be just as nice, they were compatible in size, just not as fast. He spent lots of time studying manuals and talking statistics with his dad on various aircraft. It is what he missed most; the time spent learning about all sorts of things with his father. As he chained his bike to the steel rack in the school yard, Ricky pulled up beside him. "Hey, Scotch, what's going on"? "Not much - I am whipped, and I didn't finish all my homework. Thank God I have a study module to start the day today". Ricky replied, "It ain't no thing, you're already smart. Are you still having Stephanie come over tomorrow after school"? "As far as I know, it's on. I wonder if I'll be able to get any smooches from her". "Wishful thinking bud,

let me know how that goes for you. I want all the details too"!
Scotch snapped back "Some of it might be censored".

During homeroom attendance, Sandy Wesson was marked
absent again for the fourth time this week. The talk in the
cafeteria yesterday, was that she was running away to Seattle with
her boyfriend Nick. She claimed that Seattle was where all the
cool kids drifted, to get away from it all. Nick had dropped out
of school last year. At that very moment, Sandy and Nick were
parked outside of Scotch's house instead of being at school. The
young couple sat in Nick's red 1968 COPO Camaro with a 427
to boot. They learned of the gold coins through the grapevine,
believing that they were stashed somewhere in Scotch's bedroom.
The master plan was to sit in the car just up the street until Mrs.
Chester left the house. Sandy would then sneak in through the
back and ransack the bedroom. Her boyfriend would standby
in the getaway car. They needed a little cash for their long road
trip to Washington together. They did not know how much was
there, but anything would help.

Scotch's mom Cheryl gently pulled out of the driveway, a
little earlier than usual. One quick look in the rearview mirror
to check her lipstick, and off she went, failing to notice the odd
car with two teenagers slumped down in the seats. She talked to
Dina quite a bit this morning, after Scotch left for school. She
was sobered up this morning and full of energy. She had made
up her mind, with a little convincing on behalf of her sister. She
was going to take a greyhound bus to North Dakota. She needed
to clear her head. No one would know about the trip, except
for her son and Dina. She had lots of errands to run today, most
importantly, the liquor store. She had several thin flasks that
needed to be filled for the five-and-a-half-hour bus trip, with
a couple of stops at rest areas. They could be hidden just about
anywhere. She exchanged waves with Mrs. Ricker as she passed
the neighbor's house. Annelle was peering into the back of the

old army truck, *probably stored her potatoes and onions in there....* who knows? The old woman had on a dark blue sweater, with her raggedy night gown hanging down to her boots. Cheryl lit a cigarette and headed off to town. Shortly thereafter, a freckled face girl was running beside the Chester's house, headed to the back door. Sandy opened the screen door, but the main door was locked. She peered in through the dim lit hallway and began to think. Her Dad was a senior locksmith at the Pick-A-Lock in Apple Valley. She learned some very useful things from his trade skills. If she could bust one of the small square windowpanes out, she could reach in and unlock the door. No security stickers or signs anywhere on the premises, no dogs; should be easy. As she turned towards the woods to find a rock, she was kicked in the crotch from behind so hard, she was lifted off the patio, and landed several feet away on the cement surface. The last thing she saw before being hurled into the air, was a brown foot with long dirty toes tipped with yellowing toenails, housed in a leather sandal. It came up out of nowhere from behind her. Her eyes had bright green flashes blocking her vision, she wanted to puke. That was the most pain she ever felt in her life. She had the urge to yell profanities and scream at the same time. When she looked up behind her, a tall man in a white robe looked down on her. He had to be at least seven feet tall! She tried to verbalize her thoughts of pain and hatred, but nothing came out. Her voice was nothing but a whisper. She quietly managed to get out, "What the fuck was that for asshole"! In a low dark voice, he said "You must be Sandy. I am Scotch's bodyguard. Something tells me that you are the bitch that kicked him in the crotch after your friends attacked him". "I don't know what you're talking about", she whispered back with tears in her eyes. "He calmly replied, "It's okay, that's not important". She felt a little relief, but still pissed and in terrible pain. Khalif came back, "Your day is about to get a whole lot worse cupcake". He grabbed an ornate cast iron chair that was on the back porch, the one that Cheryl liked to quietly smoke on while she watched the subtle nature in the backyard. He rotated his tall torso to one side, and snapped back in a flash, the opposite way. Sandy's bottom jaw shattered and dislocated from the top jaw after direct contact with the metal chair. Her mouth was full of broken teeth and blood. She was ready to pass out. Khalid snapped his fingers in the distance and walked back towards the cave. As Sandy lay on her side, she looked to see where he was headed. She felt a little bit of solace in a fetal position, the worst was over. Just then, the head of a large reptile, twice as big as a kickball appeared looking into her eyes. The smell was horrid, a large, forked tongue quietly whipped her face at the speed of light. The mouth opened as wide as it could, the eyes disappearing out of view. The rotten odor became intense and there was a hot humid heat warming her bloody face. The vicious head clamped down on her skull, crushing it like a pumpkin. She passed out. The snake consumed her body one inch at a time. Its body was the size of a sewer pipe. Fifteen minutes later, it slithered away towards the pond, with a red and white shoelace, hanging from the side of its mouth. With the combined weight of its body and the flesh of its meal, it rustled through the brush and snapped branches on the way back into the woods.

Nick was waiting out in the car getting more nervous as the time passed. Sandy had been gone for about 20 minutes now. An Eagan Police car was slowly coming towards him from up ahead. As it crept to a crawl parallel to his car, he noticed the windows were solid black with tint, even the windshield. Nobody was visible inside the patrol car. He rolled his window down, ready to give a phony alibi story, but the police car just kept rolling by at a crawl. As it disappeared over the hill, in his rear-view mirror, Nick pulled away from the side of the road. He headed out of the neighborhood, thinking that Sandy would catch up with him later. The urge to speed was overcome by the fear of getting busted by the cops. His suspended license and outstanding warrant could get him thrown in jail. Then he would never make it to Seattle. Out on the main road, he accelerated to the 40-mph speed limit and cranked up the stereo. Heavy Metal was his preference and he liked to listen to it loud. Suddenly, he heard a siren, the same cop car was 10 feet away from his bumper. After decelerating and pulling over to the side of the road, Nick could see the large face of the encroaching driver in his rear-view mirror. The officer had a bright white face and dark sunglasses on. There was no one else in sight. He silenced the radio and tucked his illegal pistol under the seat with his left foot, then rolled down the window. This must be some kind of a prank. The cop looked like a clown with no colored make up, just a white head and shades in a dark uniform. His mouth was just a horizontal slit on his white face with no lips. The sharp-edged police cap kept his bright blue hair tucked up inside. The deformed man angled his body towards Nick and slowly bent down. His breath reeked of rotten meat. "Can I help you officer"? The strange gentleman replied in an authoritarian voice, "I was given information that you were involved in a scuffle with Scotch Chester down at the high school". "No sir, I was just a bystander in that". A lion's roar suddenly came from the deepest part of the officer's esophagus, followed by "License and registration please"! As Nick handed him his invalid license and a folded-up piece of paper from the glove box, he had every intention to speed off, and not ever slowing down until he reached Seattle. Before he could process what was happening, the cop grabbed his arm and pulled him out through the car window with incredible strength. Scrapes, bruises, and sprains were felt all at once. He was slammed to the ground as a black Billy Club shattered every finger on his right hand. The officer had Nick's full attention now. He then sternly yelled, "Do you remember now, stepping on Scotch's fingers? "Yes, I remember now but…. The officer lifted Nick up by the neck and effortlessly tossed him to the side of the road like a rag doll. The cop looked to both sides, to make sure no one was around. Nick lay on the ground motionless, with one black eye staring at the officer. The bullet exited the officer's pistol like lightning and went right through the center of Nick's forehead. The man in the dark uniform quickly dragged Nick's body to the back of the patrol car and deposited it into the trunk with a thud. He slammed the trunk closed with lots of force, not seeming to have a care in the world. The clown cop walked swiftly back to the kid's red car with the heavy metal music still playing, much softer now. He reached in the open window with his black leather hands and turned the key off. He threw the ring of keys far into the woods. The shiny key chain "SEATTLE OR BUST" would lay in the thick weeds for years to come. On his way back to the patrol car, he examined the ground for any blood. Nothing, it was a clean site. He picked up his casing and climbed in the car. The blue flashers were turned off and he drove off quietly and orderly.

After school on that Thursday afternoon, Scotch rode his bike home. He was thinking about his date with Stephanie tomorrow, and the excitement made his legs pump harder as he stood high on the pedals. His bike sped up to top speed. The wind blew his hair back, he never felt so good! He realized he never got permission from his mom or even told her about a girl coming to the house. He would have to figure all that out tonight. Meeting Stephanie at the library could be a last resort back up plan. The whole ordeal would be a lot more fun in his own backyard though. The boy glided up the hill of the driveway tapering off his excessive speed toward the open garage, dismounted and leaned the bike against the wall of the garage. He slung his book bag off one shoulder and grabbed one of the padded straps with the opposite hand. He noticed his mother's car was in the garage, but her seldomly used bicycle was missing. The two steel brackets on the garage wall were empty. *She hasn't taken that thing out in years; hope she still has enough balance to ride it.* As he entered the house through the garage, a sheet of white paper laid by itself in the middle of the island counter in the kitchen. He picked up the lined notebook paper and read his mom's writing.

Scotch,

I have decided to take a trip to Minot to visit Aunt Dina. There is a lot going on in my mind, I did not tell you half of it when we spoke yesterday. I will be home after a few days. Took my bike to the bus station to save on parking. Please get the mail and take the trash out on Tuesday. And do not forget to brush your teeth. I am leaving you $40, there are plenty of leftovers in the freezer. Take good care son, we will talk some more when I get back. Love Always, Mom

Like he did not see that coming. What *did* surprise him though, was that he did not think a trip out West would happen so quickly. *Well, that takes care of tomorrow's date with Steph. No need to conjure up some story to present to his mother for approval. Life is good!* His thinking was interrupted by the drone of the mail truck with the Chevy S10 motor, pulling away from the mailbox out front, with a generous amount of foot pressure to the gas pedal. He guzzled some milk out of the refrigerator and headed out front to the mailbox. There were several letters, mostly junk mail and a weekly flyer with coupons of unknown products that some other people might buy. He noticed a large branch laying across the side lawn of his property, over by Mrs. Ricker's. Scotch laid the mail on the brick ledge next to the garage door and proceeded to retrieve the branch. The dead branch must have blown down during the gusty storm the other night. From far up the street, a car came to a screeching halt. The driver must have been hauling ass, judging from the sound of the skidding tires. It looked like Mrs. Ricker's Cadillac. The engine roared back to life as the tires peeled out. The front end lifted high into the air and tilted to the right. The large silver car accelerated to a high rate of speed, five times the neighborhood speed limit. It rushed towards his direction and decisively careened sideways, taking out Annelle's mailbox with a large crash and blasting into several pots of recently purchased mums. The car accelerated from a stop up the driveway towards the open garage. The interior looked to be engrossed in flames and heavy black smoke! He could not see the driver. It skidded to a stop in the garage and went silent as the engine cut out with a backfire; the blast sounding like a shotgun. As Scotch ran with panic through the hedge to see what was going on, he just caught sight of the bottom garage door panel slowly kissing the concrete. WHAT THE HELL JUST HAPPENED? Her house would be burned to the ground in minutes. He checked the side door, locked. He ran to the front door, locked. He sprinted across both yards, into his garage and into the kitchen as fast as his legs would take him. He grabbed for the phone so quick, he almost ripped the whole phone off the wall. He dialed 911. As he put the receiver to his head, he realized the line was dead. He ran to the living room, picked up that phone......also dead. He took a deep breath, grabbed a sledgehammer out of the garage and ran for Mrs. Ricker's back door. Just then, he noticed her back door ajar. As he approached and slowed down, he heard someone say something. Scotch was huffing and puffing while out of breath. He could see the tip of her nose and chin just past the edge of the door. A little bit of gray hair blew in the breeze from the side of her head. In her sweetest softest voice, she asked "Scotch, how would you like to come in for some fresh biscuits and some sweet tea? I just made them, and I have someone that would love to meet you. I think she has a crush on you". Scotch loosened his grip on the handle and the heavy hammer fell to the ground. He slowly walked in a dazed confusion towards the neighbor's door. Calmly, she spoke again. "Just give me a minute while I get my housecoat, wait right here". As Scotch came within a few feet of the door, the door slowly closed almost all the way with an eerie creak. While he waited, he examined the area of the garage. No smoke, no noise. The only sound was that of a late season cicada bug buzzing in the treetops. The loud sound was moving, but at a very slow pace. As usual, he could not locate the bug. He looked over into the woods behind his house. He could see the pond, the woodpile and the firepit. The opening to the ground or her aluminum ladder could not be seen from here. That was a relief. Why wasn't he smelling any smoke by now from her garage. The inside of the Cadillac was engulfed in flames and heavy black smoke when he saw it last. Who was driving the dam thing? It might be worth the time to break into the garage and have a look. Suddenly, he heard Annelle yell from her kitchen. "Alright, come on in kid, the door is open". Scotch gently pulled the storm door open; the inside door was already wide open. He wondered who this person is that has a crush on him, and it was a "she". *This old woman is insane, what kind of story is she conjuring up? Am I getting myself into a dangerous situation?* Suddenly, out of nowhere came a large dark shadow encroaching towards him. It was a large Doberman with its mouth snapping and raging; sharp white teeth moving up and down with assertion. Its large black glossy eyes were fixated on Scotch's face. As it lurched towards him, a long chain ratcheted over the top stair of the basement. The loud mechanical noise was being overtaken by the growls from within the dog's jaws. Speed and momentum were evident from the claws scraping the linoleum floor for traction and the bony parts of the dog's legs hitting the walls and the kitchen furniture. The dog seemed to grow immensely in size every millisecond that it approached. In an instant, the chain tightened and nearly choked the animal. It stopped the dog inches away from Scotch's nose. Saliva flung forward out of its jaws. He could smell the dogfood on its breath as it swung from side to side, its head rotating violently trying to break the chain. It had a milky white slobber all around its mouth. This dog wanted to kill him! Scotch could hardly breathe, and his heart was pounding a mile a minute. As he stepped back towards the door, Mrs. Ricker came from the kitchen. She raised her finger and yelled "Precious…. now, now. Don't worry Scotty, he won't hurt you". The dog lost its stiff form, hunkered down, reversed direction, and disappeared down the basement stairway with the loose chain dragging behind him, one link at a time dropping over the top of the stairs. *This old lady definitely has something strange and unique about her ways.*

Mrs. Ricker looked cleaned up and younger today. "I'm sorry, I forgot she was up from her nap. Hope she didn't frighten you. Have a seat over there on the couch, make yourself at home". The dog just about crushed him in the jaws of its mouth, and she is acting like it was nothing but a nuisance event. The chaos was replaced with a peaceful serenity as he entered a new room. The living room looked meticulous. The ornate furniture was dust free and polished with shiny lemon polish. The sofa and two armchairs were covered with soft white sheets with colorful accent pillows neatly placed everywhere possible. The room was filled with a fragrant flower smell, overpowering the antiquity of the place. There were a couple of large, scented candles burning on the coffee table. *This was nice.* Soft island music drifted from the old fabric speakers of her antique stereo with the phonograph player turning away inside. The old woman went to the top of the basement stairs. "Amy, are you coming up, Scotch is here"! A young voice answered back, "I'll be right up Ma, just watching the last couple of minutes of my show". Scotch could not believe what he was witnessing. *Was this a strange dream, or was it real? Never knew the lady had a dog, not to mention a daughter that he was about to meet with a sweet-sounding voice. She is probably some scary looking orphan, with scars and bruises. She probably hadn't showered in a couple of weeks and wearing baggy prison overalls, covered in dog hair. This must be the mental daughter that Mr. and Mrs. Ricker adopted and supposedly sent her off to the funny farm upstate. Had she graduated from the institute and sent back home?*

Annelle was back in the kitchen, he could hear her stirring the iced tea in a glass pitcher with a wooden spoon, humming a little melody to herself. A girl appeared at the top of the stairs. Scotch's jaw dropped. She was gorgeous! She had a tanned complexion and long black silky hair flowed over her shoulders. Her lips were thick and luscious, and her big brown eyes gazed into his. She had beautiful round cheeks and a smile from ear to ear. Her perfectly aligned teeth were as white as could be. Amy had on tight faded denim shorts with white fringe hanging from the edges. Her long legs were slightly muscular with a glossy shine to them. She had on a tight white t-shirt with a perfect bosom, nipples barely visible pointing up and out. A little bit of natural cleavage in the V-neck of her shirt finished off her look. With no hesitation, she came over to where he was sitting, and plopped down next to him, very closely. He could feel the warmth of her skin brushing against his legs. The smell of soap and perfume surrounded her body. Her eyes never left his from the top of the stairs. "Hi, I'm Amy. I finally get to meet my neighbor"! "I'm Scotch, it's a pleasure to meet you". She placed her warm hand on his bare inner thigh sliding just beneath the edge of his shorts, leaned away, and kicked off her soft fuzzy slippers. She tucked one leg underneath the other and leaned back towards him. Annelle suddenly appeared from the kitchen with a plate loaded up with steaming biscuits. The aroma of cinnamon was out of this world. She placed two plates down on the coffee table. "I made some biscuits for you kids, let me grab the sweet tea". "Yummy, my favorite!", exclaimed Amy. She giggled and lifted one of the biscuits to Scotch's lips. "Careful, it might be hot sweetie". Her hand went back on his thigh. He hoped that nobody would see his erection beneath his loose-fitting shorts. Annelle returned with some glasses and a pitcher of iced tea. "I hope you two don't mind, I experimented with the tea a little bit. I decided to add some fresh raspberries from my brother's farm to spruce things up a little". Mrs. Ricker went to the chair across from them. The sweet tea was a perfect complement to the desserts. How could two simple things taste out of this world like never before? *Mrs. Ricker surely had some skill…and secrets.* The conversation was soothing and relaxing, mostly small talk while the three of them got to know each other. A color TV in the corner of the room was flipped on at some point with a quiet soap opera on. It was easy to look over at, when Scotch was unable to answer a difficult question from Mrs. Ricker; either he didn't know the answer, or he just felt that it was none of her business. It also gave Amy a chance to rub her soft hand up and down Scotch's leg when her mother wasn't looking. At one point over the two-hour period, Scotch asked the old woman how she liked her Cadillac. "Old Betsy is a beautiful machine; she gets me to a lot of places. I think she needs a tune-up though, smells like a little smoke coming from the tailpipe". Scotch tried his best to prevent bursting out with laughter, as he had the vision of the billowing inferno within the Cadillac. Later that day, Scotch did not remember much of what they talked about. He was so entranced with this beautiful girl, that none of it mattered. It was like he was sitting in heaven that day. He never felt like that in his life, and he wanted more of it. A lot more. As things finished up, he crossed the neighbor's backyard over to his house. He grabbed the sledgehammer off the lawn and headed for the larger opening in the hedge (less briars) that he found earlier. He could not help looking at the massive truck beneath the shade trees. It had the look of evil, strength, and power. At that moment, he prayed that the soul of the truck would never come to life again. It probably had many secrets. *What role did this vehicle play in the war? How many lives did it see perish? Did it collect carcasses from the trenches?* Someday, he would maybe learn more. There was a cloud around him of some sort, he was not sure if he was in a dream. He was lightheaded and fuzzy. He pinched himself and felt it, but that could have been part of the dream as well. He remembered to retrieve the mail that he left at the front of the house on the brick ledge. Into the house he went, with a little skip to his step. The mail was tossed onto the kitchen counter, where his mom could easily see it when she returned from her trip. After heating up some frozen lasagna, he decided to retire to bed early. Tomorrow was going to be a big day. Steph was going to meet him at the firepit at 5 pm. She did not talk about it much at school this week to him, but he figured it gave a little more secrecy to their new romance. If she never showed up, it would be her loss. He had Amy now, his incredible next-door neighbor.

EIGHT

LONG AWAITED FRIDAY

THE ALARM WENT OFF AT the usual time. Scotch jumped out of bed. Friday had arrived, one more day of school until the weekend. But today was the big day. Would Stephanie show up, or will it be a forgotten promise? Breakfast was not a top priority today. Some orange juice, and the last brownish-yellow banana would have to do. A thorough shave with a new razor started the process. Dad left behind a can of Old Spice shaving cream. It had a little bit of rust on the top rim of the can, but it would still suffice. Next was a long shower, using a bar of deodorant soap that he got last year in his Christmas stocking. He dried off quickly letting his towel fall to the floor, he was running behind. He uncoiled the hair dryer and brushed back his brown hair. Normally, he would let his hair air dry on the bike ride to school. It was amazing how the hair dryer added a feathery look and a special shine to his golden-brown hair, especially when using the stylist brush instead of a comb. A little hairspray to hold the waves, and he was satisfied. He had picked out an outfit the night before and slipped it on as quick as he could. In no time, he was off to school.

He realized he wasn't that behind on time after all, so he decided to take the route by the airport. As he approached the fence, a red and white biplane was barreling down the runway under full power. The colorful contraption leaped off the runway and accelerated at a steep angle into the bright blue sky. As he banked the plane towards Scotch's direction, the boy could clearly make out the pilot's face. He blinked twice; it was that of a rabbit. He saw its face very clearly. It had a brown leather jacket, chrome encased goggles, a leather cap, and a white wispy scarf. The rabbit's laughter could be heard over the roar of the engine. Scotch turned his bike away from the fence and raced off towards to school. His legs were wobbly by the time he arrived in the schoolyard.

Homeroom was uneventful. He finished up on a take-home quiz for his first period class. Once again, Sandy was absent. He was beginning to think that she was settling down in Seattle by now with her boyfriend Nick. She was just another one of the bullies at school. He was not going to miss her threats and rhetoric. He talked to Ricky about coming over to the house on Saturday. Scotch needed some help lifting a large trunk into the garage. Ricky was already filled in on the details of the possible treasure, he gladly accepted. The boys planned to do some fishing after that. The day at school dragged on slowly, he already missed his mom. Stephanie was nowhere to be seen, making him feel a little uncomfortable with all his beauty prep that morning. Some of his classmates made fun of him a little bit at lunch with his new look. Friday was pizza day in the cafeteria, it seemed to lift everybody's spirits a little bit. Scotch took all the taunting throughout the morning lightly. After school, he went out to the bike rack, unchained his bicycle, and began the short trek home. After a light snack of cheese doodles and a coke at the kitchen counter, he headed up to his room to complete his homework for Monday. Before he was finished, the B747

simulator was calling his name. He messed around with it until 4:30. It was time to head down back to start the fire, just in case she showed up. He decided to start the fire with soft wood, before introducing the harder oak. He picked out five of the best-looking birch logs and gathered some small sticks and grass from around the shore of the pond. Before he knew it, the fire was ablaze, with three-foot flames lapping at the sky. Not much sparking going on from moisture; covering the wood with canvas always paid off. His father taught him many great things like that. Some motion caught his attention up towards the back of the house. It was Stephanie! She was smiling as she walked down the path towards him, zig zagging back and forth, her arms flailing in the air. She was talking with a happy voice; he couldn't quite hear what she was saying because of the crackling fire. As she got closer, Scotch realized she was all dressed up. She had light brown suede hiking boots on, appropriate for the woods. They made her look quite sexy. Shiny red latex leggings looked like they were painted onto her beautiful figure, topped off with a fluffy white angora sweater. She was wearing bright red lipstick, and her eye makeup looked amazing! Scotch was careful to play things cool. Afterall, this meeting was to work on their history projects for next week. "Hey Steph, how are you doing"? "I'm doing quite well now that the weekend is finally here. Nice fire you got going there". As she was coming around the woodpile, she lost her footing and tripped over something. She was able to catch herself before committing to a complete fall. "Careful there, are you okay? Have a seat on the rustic bench where it will be safer for you". Scotch joined her. They both sat on the huge log that was about 7 feet long. It was free of bark and the planed top half was well worn from lots of sitting over the years. The thick coat of varnish that Mike applied years ago, was holding up just fine. It made for a shiny, splinter-free surface suitable for any attire. They had a comfortable conversation for a while, gazing at the flames of the warm fire. Steph pulled out a pack of cigarettes and lit one up with a bright red lighter. Scotch didn't comment, he wanted her to stay relaxed. They talked some more, and Steph entertained the thought of smuggling a couple of drinks out of his mom's liquor cabinet. "How did you know we have a liquor cabinet"? "Every house with normal people living in it, has some sort of liquor cabinet". "Well, we do have some schoolwork to do, how about we save it for another time"? "Well, I thought we could just talk out some ideas, then write it up on our own, and maybe meet again in a few days to polish them up". She was reaching into her pocketbook again, grabbing for her pack of cigarettes. This time she pulled out what looked like a large marijuana joint. "I didn't know you smoked Steph". "I only smoke a little weed, after I have a cigarette". He laughed, "So you only smoke when you smoke"! "Yeah, something like that, do you want to join me"? "I don't smoke cigarettes; they make me wheeze. But I like a little doobage on occasion". This was a total lie. Scotch never had a cigarette before, and he was never exposed to any weed. He figured if he was ever going to try the forbidden stuff, right now would be the perfect opportunity, to show this beautiful girl that he was cool and laid back. Before he could answer her offer, she was already stoking the end with the lighter. A large cloud of smoke covered her face. He could see a bright smile through it all. She passed the white stick to him, smeared with a little bit of red lipstick. Scotch grabbed the joint and took a puff. He immediately coughed a couple of times. "I should have warned you; this weed is a little stronger than usual. Comes up from Panama. Here try this". She slid herself closer to him on the log, and faced him directly, just a few inches away. He turned sideways and straddled the log to match her image. Her legs were spread wide so that her body could be close, contacting the outside of his knees to the insides of hers. She took the joint, turned it around and put the lit end in her mouth.

She sealed her shiny red lips around it and began to exhale. A fine horizontal column of smoke streamed from the joint, as she pulled him closer. He realized how this was supposed to work now. He inhaled the column of smoke like he was an expert. Awesome, no cough this time. She smiled and replied in the coolest voice, "It's called a French hit". The two of them finished the fat doober, until there was just a tiny roach left. Scotch felt wasted, but relaxed and humored. Stephanie pulled something else out of her bag. It was a roach clip with a braided green rope and a small yellow pom pom dangling on the end of the short rope. Each of them had one more hit before the small ember was released to the fire. They talked a little bit more before the idea of drinking came up again. Scotch said, "Alright, you twisted my arm enough, let's go take a look up in the cabinet, see what we find". "Scotch, you go up, I'll wait here. I'll have another cigarette and tend to the fire". "Okay, what's your poison going to be"? "I love brandy, schnapps and I'll drink any kind of red wine". "Sounds good, I'll try to get something for us to eat too". Right then, she stood up from the log bench and wrapped her arms around him. She connected her lips to his and began to kiss him. Her shiny red leggings were pressed against his body as she slowly moved up and down his body arousing him instantly. He tried to act natural and suddenly she slipped the tip of her tongue into his mouth. He did the same and they kissed forever, maybe almost a minute. They separated and both smiled at each other. Scotch realized he was high as a kite. He giggled and turned towards the house. She fumbled in her bag for another cigarette. On his way up to the back door, he realized that he never told Steph that his mother was away until the middle of next week. Maybe he could convince her to stay over tonight. For now, he was concentrating on his footage. Everything seemed to happen in slow motion, and everything around him was beautiful! Even the weeds were as pretty as roses. Things were oddly different.

Stephanie kept looking towards the house. *Where the hell was Damon, he was supposed to be here by now.* Unfortunately, he was at home sound asleep. He laid down for a few minutes after school, which turned into hours. The cocaine that he snorted and the two shots of tequila, probably made him a little drowsier than he expected.

Scotch found a good rock n' roll station on the living room stereo. He cranked it up and began to gather up the goods. There was a fresh block of Vermont sharp cheddar cheese in the fridge that needed to be sliced up. An unopened box of fancy crackers was in the cupboard. As he looked through the liquor cabinet, he found a pint of blackberry brandy and a larger bottle of peppermint schnapps that was more than half full. Mom did not fancy either of these, otherwise, they would have been gone. She would not even know the bottles were missing. He grabbed a canvas tote bag with sturdy handles and began to fill it up. A couple of paper plates, napkins, and a couple of thick glass tumblers. He even threw a couple of twinkies in there. He seemed to have a strong craving for those right now. It wouldn't hurt to throw the last three in the box in there as well, finish them up. He was trying to divide five by two; he couldn't do it. The cheese knife was nowhere to be found. Perhaps, he should check on the shelves down in the basement where the less used party utensils, and larger pots and pans lived.

Meanwhile, Stephanie wandered over to the cave area that Scotch pointed out to her earlier. She saw the aluminum ladder leading down into the crevice. She wasted no time in retrieving her dad's new halogen flashlight out of her pocketbook. She began to descend the ladder, one rung at a time. Reaching the bottom, she followed the trail into the darkness. Her beam of light scanned back and forth ahead of her. This cave was a lot bigger than she had imagined. Up ahead, a dark wooden chest appeared, she quickened her pace towards it, nervous as could be.

This must be it! As she looked around, all was quiet amidst the musty cool air. She got down on one knee to figure out the latch with the small flashlight in her mouth. As she reached towards it and touched it with her fingertips, the top of the latch just fell downwards, dangling by one attachment point at the bottom. She grabbed both sides of the large heavy trunk top and jimmied it with all her might until the top came free. The top half of the trunk hinged open, held by two thick leather straps. Steph leaned it against the dirt wall. She just about had a heart attack. The trunk was filled completely with shiny gold coins…. thousands of them. There it was - the infamous treasure that the Chester kid bragged about for days…. for real! How was she going to get it out of here? Bags of coins at a time, the whole thing at once…. shit, she would need a crane. Suddenly she felt scared. This is a dangerous situation; people would kill over this treasure. As she stood up, she bumped into a body standing behind her. As she turned to face him with her flashlight in hand, it was a tall thin giant man in a long white robe. "Who are you"? she exclaimed in a shaky voice. He grabbed her by the throat with one warm hand and lifted her two feet off the ground. She tried to scream, but nothing came out. With the other hand, he grabbed one of her ankles and flipped her upside down. As she hung suspended in air, he grabbed the other ankle and spread her legs apart. His long arms gave him a very wide span. Her loud scream was muffled by the depths of the cave. A popping sound followed by extreme pain put her into instant shock. She blacked out. Khalif had just dislocated both legs from her hips. He dropped her body to the ground face first. He grabbed both of her wrists and raised them hard and sharply. There were two snaps, her young bones giving away under the extreme strength of the powerful man. He placed his size 13 leather sandal on the small of her back. He bent over and grabbed her long blond hair, one quick yank upwards and most of her hair tore from her skull, but not before her neck cracked in two. He dropped the worthless carcass on the ground. Snake would find this one later. For now, he sensed Damon coming into the quiet neighborhood. He would have to act fast to orchestrate his next move. After ascending the ladder with lightning speed, he made his way up the path, leading to the back of the house. It was starting to get dark. The back door opened, the rock music from within got louder. Next the screen door opened, and Scotch stepped out onto the concrete patio. He toted a canvas bag and a bottle of red wine in his free hand. His cheery face had a smile from ear to ear. He had a corkscrew in his front pocket. His eyes locked on to Khalif's eyes. Suddenly, everything became serious. Scotch placed the bag on the wrought iron chair. He didn't notice Sandy's blood covering one of the legs of the chair. A conversation without words began to flow. The magical being was going to borrow Scotch's body. Scotch would be transformed into a small animal for a short time. In a low calm voice Khalif replied, "Stephanie left for home to get some more weed, Panama Red. She will be back a little later". Everything was going to be fine. Suddenly, Scotch felt small. He looked around – his body was close to the ground, and he was on all fours. His vision was odd: the colors were different, and he could see a lot further with a wider span. Aromas from the woods filled his nostrils, almost too much to process – the oak leaves, mushrooms, grasses, and twigs. His muscles and his movements all felt strange. He went to see where Khalif was headed, and he found himself bouncing instead of walking, moving down the path rather quickly. He instinctively jumped onto a tree and began climbing with ease. His hands stuck to the oak tree like Velcro, he was light and nimble. He kept climbing and climbing, jumping from tree to tree. The bonfire in the distance got much bigger, flames reaching at least five feet into the dusk. *Stephanie really did a good job while he was away.* He could see Khalif approaching the log bench, only he was Scotch. *This is crazy, he has got my body on!* He looked down at his own tiny arms, they were covered in gray fur, he was now a squirrel! Scotch was distracted by some snapping of branches and rustling leaves up by the house. Somebody was approaching quickly, but not on the path. As the sound moved closer to the woodpile, he could make out Damon's face. Damon Wheeler…. what was he doing here? The squirrel lay low on the high tree branch overhead the firepit. It could not wait to see what was about to happen.

Damon approached Scotch's figurine. "Where's Stephanie, punk"? Scotch replied calmly, "She's up in my room, taking a shower. We just had sex and she wanted to freshen up a bit for the after-hour party. What brings you out here faggart, you're on private property"? Damon was fuming beyond belief. He went to punch Scotch right in the throat with all his might. Scotch lifted his own hand in a flash, and grabbed Damon's fist, bringing it to a complete stop. It made the sound of an American League fastball landing square in the center of a catcher's mitt. With one fluid movement, he rotated the fist, and twisted the arm behind Damon's back. He lifted him up off the ground by the twisted arm and snapped it right out of the shoulder socket as his injured body was thrown into the brush. Damon sprung up off the ground in pain but refusing to show any signs of defeat. "What did you enroll in some sort of hotshot karate school you little twit? You're going to pay for that little maneuver"! Damon ran at Scotch only to be met with a straight arm right to the ugly pocked nose. It was solid! As his mangled body lay hunched over, Damon could see blood dripping steadily to the ground beneath his face. He gave up, he was beat. Khalif snatched a log of oak from the top of the woodpile. As he leaned over from behind him with his arm gently placed on Damon's shoulder, he whispered, "Let me help you Damon, I'm really sorry buddy". He swung the log upwards, and it smashed into Damon's teeth, knocking several to the back of his throat. He went flying back landing in the woods once again, choking on his shattered teeth and a mouth full of blood. He was moaning loudly and crying. He could no longer get any words out. Khalif got down on one knee, grabbed a fistful of Damon's shirt and with his other hand, he thrusted the corkscrew from Scotch's shirt pocket through Damon's right eyeball. It went in as easily as penetrating a small, boiled egg. The metal coil of the appliance turned the eyeball several times. Eventually the muscular cord in the back snapped and Khalif extracted the eyeball from the head with a tight sucking sound. Damon's body went limp and quiet. The squirrel could not believe his eyes. He was excited with revenge at first, and now he felt as if he just witnessed a murder for the first time.... with one of his own classmates. He scurried down the oak tree and back up to the porch. He could no longer watch this gruesome attack. A few minutes later, Khalif appeared at the top of the path. Their eyes connected and the silent conversation began. Scotch got his body back; a squirrel ran like the wind into the bushes. Khalif put Scotch into a calm state of mind. He told the boy not to worry, he would take care of Damon's dead body and extinguish the fire. Scotch was dismissed for the night. He grabbed the tote off the chair and headed into the house. He threw the cheese in the fridge, returned the undisturbed bottles of booze to the liquor cabinet, and dragged himself up to bed. After he removed his clothes and brushed his teeth, he could not ignore the urge to look down back in the woods. There was Khalif, standing tall over the fire. There were strong rays of bluish green light from Khalif's eyes, cast down on the firepit. The flames were ten feet in the air! It was as if the stone lined fire pit was being incinerated. He suspected that Damon's body was the center of interest, the focal point to the raging fire. He returned to the bathroom. As he gazed into the mirror, he noticed that all his cuts and bruises were gone from the week before. Even his face was clear of acne. The build of his body appeared to be more defined and muscular, his hair looked perfect. He shook his head in disbelief, switched off the light and laid down in his bed. It was the last thing that he remembered. He fell asleep dreaming that Stephanie would return in the middle of the night to hold him close. He left the door unlocked out back, just in case.

NINE

A QUIET WEEKEND

SCOTCH AWOKE TO A COOL breeze blowing through the thin curtains. The shades were pulled almost all the way down. He looked over at the digital clock, it was 9:38 am. It was nice to sleep in late on a Saturday morning for a change. He dreamed of Stephanie lying next to him throughout the night, her slippery red legs entwined around his body. As he slowly got up and got dressed next to his empty bed, he thought about the day ahead. Scotch's mind didn't have the strength to figure out the events of the past few days- everything was a little too crazy right now. He needed to meet up with Ricky and then check out this trunk from days gone by if it was even still there. Then he needed to return Mrs. Ricker's ladder, after he gave it a thorough cleaning. The nylon rope needed to be repaired to fulfill the promise that he made to himself. After looking down back from the bedroom window, he was convinced that the fire was out cold. The pit was empty of ashes and no sign of smoke whatsoever. He knew from Amy's conversation last Thursday, that she and Mrs. Ricker were going to visit some relatives on a Wisconsin farm for a few days. They left Friday morning. *Home schooling must be nice,* he thought. If the trunk was still there, he needed to find out what was inside. If there was anything of value, he needed to hoist it out of there, and bring it up to the garage where it would be safe. Dad had some old block and tackle hanging up in the garage with two milk crates full of the finest hemp rope. The Parks Department left a message for the Chester Family on the answering machine in the living room about filling in the dangerous hole next week before winter was upon Minnesota. No one needed to be present for the work.

He wondered about Mom as he stared at her empty chair across the dimly lit room. She was in good hands with Aunt Dina, as long as drugs and alcohol weren't going to be involved during their therapy session. He thought to himself, those crazy childhood days are coming to an end for the aging women. The boy eavesdropped in on many stories over the years. Mom still likes her alcohol, but it cannot last forever. The sisters are grown up; life is more serious with lots of responsibilities and fewer problems. Aunt Dina will fix her up. He really felt this in his heart.

As he was browning up some sausage links that were resting in a puddle of butter, the kitchen started to smell like the old days. Mom loved making breakfast for the three of them on the weekends, no matter what was on the schedule or how little food there was in the fridge to work with. Some fried eggs over easy would be laid onto some fresh english muffins. They were just starting to turn golden brown in the toaster oven. With fresh Maxwell coffee brewing in the pot, life didn't get much better. After things were under control, he decided to go out on the patio and smoke one of his mother's cigarettes on this beautiful crisp Saturday morning. It would give him a quiet chance to observe the woods down back, from a distance. Ricky was planning to stop by around 11am. The doorbell interrupted his train of thought. *Who the heck is at the front door on a Saturday? Too early for Ricky, he usually shows up late. Is it one of those religious groups, or someone like a roof repair guy?* He snuffed out the cigarette and ran into the house. He wiped his hands off with the nearest towel. Free of butter and pork grease, he made his way to the front door. *This better be quick.* He turned the dead bolt and pulled the door open. What a surprise, Billy Preston the greaseball stood before him. "What can I do for you Billy"? "Hey, is your mom around"? "No, she isn't, and I think it is a very bad idea for you to come around here". "Oh yeah, why is that"? "Because you're a loser, and I just don't think you're fit for my mother". "Well thanks for your opinion you little shit, tell her I stopped by, and watch your back my friend. I've got people that can set you in your place with just a phone call". "Whatever". He slammed the door, locked the deadbolt, and returned to his gourmet breakfast. What a poor excuse for a human being. Dad said that the man never got further in his career than the sewer treatment plant. *What a shitty job that must be.*

Billy rounded the corner of the Chester's house. He followed the path between their house and Mrs. Ricker's. He never trusted the old Ricker witch. She was always spying on the neighbors it seemed. He stopped to take a leak on the old GMC Army truck.

While he was urinating in the chosen spot, he noticed that the damn tires came up to his chest. As he zipped up and walked away, he planned his day out. That little shit of a kid made him angry. How dare he interfere with he and Cheryl's love squad? Billy made up his mind. Yesterday was payday, he's headed to Grandma Poodle's house on the other side of town. She was an elderly woman who supplied all the drugs to the locals. She was sharp as a whip and did not trust anyone. She was extremely cautious and stealthy in her old age, and of course, she had a headful of tight curly gray locks, like a toy poodle. This lucky man was going to score a few grams of coke and a bag of sinsemilla. It would drift him through his week of misery, with a substantial price that he couldn't necessarily afford. A nutritious supply of food for his lanky body and money for the bills that were due would have to be put on the back burner once again. As he passed cluelessly within 20 yards of the hidden cave, he was unaware of the force that was watching him.

Khalif observed Billy's mind closely. He knew that this person was a dirtbag. Khalif came up through the Earth with his group of dependable supporters. They could transform into any shape or form, and they precisely fixed problems as a team under the direction of the tall man. Their mission was to protect Scotch and his mother, no matter what extremes they had to take. At that moment, Preston was slated to go.

Scotch was beginning to figure things out from his angle. All these strange creatures that didn't belong in Minnesota, all the crazy events that continue to happen. He felt that the spirit of his own father had something to do with this. The whole group of strangers in the cave appeared to be of Middle Eastern descent. When Scotch's father was ambushed, he was fighting for his life and his Country over in the desert region, protecting the local Afghanistan residents from the Taliban. Khalif and his group seemed to have arrived from their homeland, planting themselves in Scotch's backyard to return the favor. They were here to destroy any threats to the Chester Family. Victims of war have come and gone throughout the history of man, and sometimes unexplained mysteries happen along the way. Only the facts find their way into the factual textbooks, the rest are just fluffed off as conspiracies. Nobody would ever believe the boy's stories. When Khalif determines that it is safe for everyone, they will reverse their underground ship, and head back to the Middle East. Until then, it would be a large test for the young Chester boy. He would have to prove himself by taking chances and impelling bravery. Every fear and phobia would need to be overcome. Scotch felt this purpose, and he was up for the challenge.

Mustafa would be the man of the day on this quiet and peaceful Saturday. His name is derived from ancient times, meaning "The chosen one". Khalif knew that Mustafa would have a little magic of his own up his sleeve to add to the mission. Mustafa exited the cave without use of the aluminum ladder. His body levitated to the surface in a slow rotation. He wore mirrored shades and donned a million-dollar smile, dressed as a biker gang banger to mix in with the population. His feet were donned with large black riding boots. They were decorated with chrome bling and matching chains, the tops of the boots covered by his faded Wrangler jeans. His beard, mustache and red bandanna completed the image. He made his way through the woods towards the large GMC in Mrs. Ricker's side yard. He had very explicit instructions from the morning meeting in the cave. There would be a small window of opportunity for this plan to work; he was the best man for the job. He approached the large military vehicle and unlatched the hood on the left side of the engine compartment. He hinged the creaky metal covering upward and rested it all the way back. He cleared out some field mouse debris and removed some access panels around the engine with the twist of a ratchet wrench. Reaching into his dark leather vest, he removed a canister of potion. He squirted it into various places, and then latched the cowling shut. He climbed into the driver's seat, sitting high and proud in the cab. His body twisted in the old, hardened seat. It was lined with a network of fine cracks from aging in the sun. It wasn't very comfortable. He turned the tarnished brass key left in the ignition and began to crank over the engine. The pistons pumped their hardest, many belts and wheels turned against friction from lack of use. Suddenly, the two overhead stacks belched out plumes of black smoke, and the old proud GMC 270 engine came to life. The flappers over the pipes seemed to prevent the smoke from escaping as they tapped up and down nervously. They suddenly gave in and were forced to be held wide open from the dominant exhaust, releasing years of dormant stillness from the engine. The struggling of sounds turned into a purring beast. The black smoke thinned to a softer light gray color. Mustafa pushed on the stiff clutch, jammed the shifter into reverse and let up on the clutch.

The gears grinded with protest. He pushed the clutch in immediately. Next, he double clutched it with a couple of perfectly timed pumps, and the old Warner T93 5-speed began to back towards the street. Mustafa was careful to minimize damage to the undisturbed earth beneath his large radials, turning the wheel ever so slightly – less to cover up later, after the mission. Twigs snapped; pine needles turned upwards. Overhead branches curved out of the way while hanging on to the vehicle, then whipping back into place as the truck released them. It was a miracle that this vehicle could ever move again under its own power. John Ricker started it in the late Fall of 1957, one last time. It was positioned into its present spot and given up on, many times over. Now, it was breathing and full of power for a day out on the town, that laid ahead for the machine and the mysterious operator.

Billy was returning from another familiar sales transaction with Grandma Poodle. He decided on an eight ball of the magic white powder instead of just a couple of grams. The score would be in the 3-to-3.5-gram range. He tried a little sample in the old lady's kitchen. It was good stuff. He didn't sense any of the lacing that the new generation was cutting into the Columbian product. Those unnecessary additives made the drug more dangerous to the consumer and more lucrative for the dealers. During his journey back home, he turned off Yankee Doodle Road to the quieter Elrene Road, he felt stoked. He would get reunited with Cheryl soon, might even share a little bit of the hooch with her. As he made his way back to the neighborhood, he increased the volume on his Hi-Fi stereo. It was as if he was in the leather bucket seat of a sleek Ferrari, but from the outside, he was in a wimpy purple 1970 AMC Gremlin. It had a white racing stripe on the sides, to add to the embarrassing look. He was cruising along on the straightaway, pushing 47 in a 40-mph speed limit. His left knee was keeping the steering wheel steady, his hands were busy rolling a joint. He was concentrating on removing a couple of seeds and a twig from his creased rolling paper, leaving behind the fresh green clumps of bud. As he momentarily glanced up, the only vehicle coming at him in the mile ahead was just a large dark truck, its faded yellow headlights uselessly shining nowhere in the daylight. *Cool, no cops up ahead.* He continued the task of rolling the doober. With the loud rock music blaring out of the woofers and the distracting task at hand, he failed to see the truck's pipes starting to belch black smoke high into the air, Mustafa was pushing the gas pedal to the floor. He had it cranked into overdrive 5th gear with the speedometer pegged at 45. As he approached the purple target, he quickly swerved to the left and back to the right. The truck just about dropped its 2 ½ ton body onto its left side before impact. The large Coker Radial tires up righted the momentum of the truck. They rode up and over the hood of the Gremlin, forcing the structure of the truck back to its upright stance on the back side of the car. It crushed the vehicle with an immense bounce through the windshield, ripping off the roof that hooked on Mustafa's chassis and exited the deformed object just behind the driver's rear door jam. Glass shattered and spewed everywhere, metal was twisted and torn. Mustafa skidded to a stop 20 yards away surrounded with smoke, the smell of rubber, oil, and gas. The truck's engine returned to a quieter idle.

He swung open the door laughing at the top of his lungs with success, the AC/DC still playing loudly on the crackling speakers. The tough bastard climbed out of the cab and examined the purple wreck. Billy was smooshed beyond recognition. His body was pancaked under the caved in roof; severed organs covered with blood were smooshed into the floorboards. Mustafa did a quick walk around inspection. The rear axle and wheels of the car were in good shape, the trunk was popped open though. The laughing man jumped back into the cab with the energy of a young athlete. He ran his hand through his long greasy hair and adjusted the toothpick sticking out the corner of his dried lips. After jamming the clutch in with his black leather boot, he slapped the shifter into first gear, he pulled further away from the purple wreck, then shifted the beast into reverse. The gears grinded away as he slowly maneuvered the massive truck around and past the wreck. After executing a perfect 180 degree turn in reverse, he exited the cab and lifted the green military tarp aside on the back of the GMC. He grabbed the 20-foot rusty chain that John Ricker was kind enough to leave behind. He slid under the Gremlin on his back and began to do his quick handywork under the front of the car's axle. The free end of the chain was connected to a steel cable with a clevis. The cable fed through a lifting frame in the cargo hold of the truck. There was an old hydraulic crank attached to the A frame that was able to lift the front of the car just high enough to prevent it from dragging on the road. When that was complete, he took Mrs. Ricker's old straw broom out of the back and swept broken glass to the side of the road. He picked up the larger pieces of the wreckage and tossed them into Billy's trunk. A little bit of fluid was in the road, but other than that, it was a clean site. There was nobody in sight to witness the carnage. He jumped up into the cab, quickly did a 180, and headed in his original direction to the local junkyard. It was gratifying that the event took place on a stretch of Elrene Road, aligned with only woods and fields, no houses yet. The traffic was always light on the weekends.

As he turned the truck onto Yankee Doodle Road, he passed by the main gate of the Ghaffi Junkyard. He could barely make out the fat security guard in his small shack, set back quite aways from the main drag. Outside the security shack, just inside of the fence, was parked a shiny red Camaro. There was a sheet of paper taped to the outside of the window. It read:

UNPROCESSED

Towed from Elrene Road, 09/18
Abandoned Vehicle set for auction.
Lack of ownership information.
Missing key.

Mustafa had no intentions of stopping here. It would be too much of a risk with the load that he was hauling. Whether it was delivering a mangled vehicle, or a junkyard hunter looking for parts, it was always a slow income to the Ghaffi Family at their junkyard. Turning in a criminal or sharing suspicious information with the local police department could easily up the ante for the business's profit margin. The guardsman felt important in his pristine uniform that his wife ironed that morning. The satisfaction of bringing in an $800 weekly salary felt like easy money for truly little work. He lived a pathetic lifestyle with no retirement. The wife lost her leg to diabetes, her future was uncertain. Their only son and the grandchildren would have to take care of the two of them someday. The security guard was caught up with his daily crossword puzzle while listening to the start of a Twins game on his transistor radio. He didn't take notice of the passing truck out on Yankee Doodle Road. Mustafa continued a mile down the road and took the first right, down a dirt road. He was welcomed with signs that said **DO NOT ENTER, PRIVATE PROPERTY** and some city codes listed at the bottom of the signs. He would only be there for a short time; it would be okay for him to enter. He travelled down the dirt road for a hundred yards or so and took another right-hand turn. A large chain link gate was in his path. It had some similar warning signs and was bound together with a chain and a padlock. The mysterious biker emerged from the truck and approached the latched gate. Through unknown powers, bluish green beams of light emitted from his eyes towards the padlock. The lock opened, the chain dropped loose, and the gate opened inwards. Mustafa climbed back into his cab and double clutched into first gear. The GMC only went a short distance before it arrived at an empty spot amongst the junk vehicles stacked several high; never even got it to second gear. In this ninety-acre lot, he was furthest away from the main gate. He drove past the spot and kicked the rig into reverse. With the help of the clad iron bumper mounted behind the GMC, he was able to force the Gremlin into the empty spot. He wobbled the shifter into neutral, set the brake, and worked the hardware free from the Gremlin's axle after lowering it to the soft powder white sand. After coiling up the cable, he decided to throw the canvas bag of stink [Mr. John Ricker] from the Army Truck into the opened trunk of the purple Gremlin. The big rig might come in handy for future missions, might as well get rid of the smelly sack of shit. He pulled away and summoned some more magic from his inner brain. He levitated a 1965 Chevy pickup from several spots away and floated it above the mangled purple Gremlin, high in the air. He released his energy, and the blue pickup crashed onto the Gremlin leaving a cloud of dust. It managed to crush the car down to the ground, concealing Billy's dead body in the front seat and sealing the trunk closed. It blended into the rows and rows of rusty steel skeletons at the Ghaffi Junkyard. As he drove out of the back entrance, Mustafa looked back at the gate. Two bluish green beams of light came from the driver's window of the Army truck. The gate swung closed, the chain wove itself back into place and the large padlock clicked to the closed position. Mustafa laughed all the way back to the neighborhood. Passing the guard shack, the attendant had his back to him as he stood over a large, opened pizza box. *Some jobs are easy and fun!* Back in the neighborhood, he slowly made his way into Annelle's yard. He parked the vehicle in the same exact position as before. After climbing out of the GMC, he removed the straw broom from the back and made the new tracks disappear beneath the pine needles. Other than scratched paint and a slightly bent fender on the driver's side, the vehicle looked undisturbed after a fun day out on the town. He returned the broom to the back, and pulled the canvas shut. The large Arab returned to the cave. The circus music played as he disappeared below the surface of the earth, in a slow descending rotation.

Ricky showed up right on time. Scotch had his Radio Flyer Town and Country Wagon waiting at the front of the garage. Ricky said, "So fill me in on the mission here, what are we going after"? "Well, I already told you, I believe there is a trunk down in this cave, next to where I found this $150 coin. I hope that the chest contains more of this treasure. Don't worry, I will give you a cut of the loot. Just between us, I think we are due for something bigger in life. I tried to move it when I first discovered it, the chest barely budged. Let's go check it out"!

When they arrived at the cave, Ricky was in awe. "Scotch, you didn't tell me it was this big! I thought we were dealing with a crack in the ground". "Yeah, well it seemed to open up a little more since the first night. The path travels underground for quite a distance too. I haven't explored the whole thing yet". The boys made their way down the ladder and into the cave. Scotch had a better flashlight this time. The trunk was still there! They opened it and grabbed handfuls of coins. They both held their hands up and released the coins back into the trunk. The sound was magnificent. Scotch explained the danger and risk of being here for too long to Ricky. The trunk had quite a bit of weight to it. Scotch saw an object lying next to the trunk. It was Stephanie's roach clip with the green rope and the yellow pom-pom. It was covered with dirt. There were also several joints in a baggie. He slipped the paraphernalia into his pocket while his friend stared up at the open hole. "Hey Ricky, give me a hand with this, would ya"! The boys managed to drag the cumbersome chest through the powdery sand using the heavy-duty side handles over to the base of the ladder. It was much too heavy to lift. Scotch had a plan in motion. It just so happened that a large oak limb was located directly above the ladder. With the block and tackle system preset into place this morning, the boys were able to heave the trunk to the surface and onto the waiting wagon. Scotch pulled with all his might, while Ricky pushed equally from the back of the wagon. Almost out of breath, they finally made it all the way up to the garage. The boys wheeled the freight around to the front of the house. After rolling it into the corner of the garage, they covered it with a large gray canvas sheet that his dad had lying around. Scotch invited Ricky into the house for a cold refreshment. "Alright Scotch, where did this treasure chest come from? Somebody must own it". Scotch replied quickly. "I don't know if you noticed, but on the inside of the chest lid, it was stenciled with 'PROPERTY OF THE U.S. ARMY'. After doing some research of the coin at the library, I may have found the trunk's origin". He slid an excerpt of his history report across the island counter towards Ricky. On the opened page, it read: The U.S. Army built Fort Snelling between 1820 and 1825 to protect American interests in the fur trade. It tasked the fort's troops with deterring advances by the British in Canada, enforcing boundaries between the region's Native American nations, and preventing Euro-American immigrants from intruding on Native American land. "During further research, there was an article written about a chest of coins that had gone missing, with the Dakota Indians listed as the main suspect. To this date, the coins were never found. My Dad talked about this old story as well". Ricky was very interested. "Should we go to the authorities with this information"? "No way my friend, the government will swarm into this quiet little neighborhood in a matter of minutes with 'confiscation in mind'. I have a gentleman in mind that will buy these coins with cash". "Well, how much is there"? Scotch answered, "One of those coins weighs around 10 grams. A thousand of them would be around 25 pounds. I'm guessing that trunk has a couple of hundred pounds. We're talking close to a million dollars, maybe more"! Ricky could not believe what he was hearing. "What do we do next Scotch"? Well, the plan is to get some of those clear coin canisters that hold dollar-size coins. We'll separate the coins into a given amount and label each of the canisters. This will make it easier to travel with them, small quantities at a time. We can work on this maybe over the next few days, let's keep it top secret though. We can set up the work bench in the garage for the project". Ricky thought he was dreaming. They headed on down back to do some fishing and share a few more stories. Before they left the kitchen though, Scotch had something else to discuss with his friend.

"Ricky, I was going through some of my mom's mail that has been gathering up since last Thursday. There was one letter that stood out. It was from the State Government. After carefully slicing it open, I read the official contents. To give you a summary of the letter, it goes like this. *Dear Property Owner: After reviewing your background, we see that you have lost your spouse who proudly served in the U.S. military. We are sorry about the circumstances, but our records at the County Office show that you have defaulted on your mortgage payments for over 6 months. This is the 5th and final notice. As of this Wednesday the 23rd day of September, you and your personal property will be removed from the premises. The alternative is to come up with the $26,356 owed by this date. If you cannot, please remove all property from the dwelling before the Sherriff's Office arrives on Wednesday. At that time, there will be no further negotiations. We regret these actions, but the State of Minnesota takes this matter very seriously. Please allow us to assist you with temporary accommodations while you sort this financial matter. Applications for needed assistance will be available on Wednesday. Have a nice day.*

"I am scared to death. My mom and I are about to lose everything. I need your help"! Ricky asked, "What can I do to help"? "I was wondering if you would travel to North Dakota with me tomorrow. I must get this urgent letter to my mom. I tried to phone her at Aunt Dina's house, but I am unable to get through. We can take the bus and be back by Monday night".

"No way Scotch. I can't do it. My aunt has bile duct cancer, and my family is going to spend some time at the hospital with her on Monday afternoon. We don't know how much time she has left. Besides, I don't even think busses run on Sundays". "Ah shit, we better get some fishing in before we run out of time".

The boys fished for a couple of hours that afternoon, they had a little bit of luck and Scotch shared stories with Ricky. He didn't believe half of them, especially about the strange men and all the unbelievable stories that took place in the woods. Ricky knew a little bit of information about the Middle East culture from a recent book report. "The black cord on the leader's head, worn doubled, is used to keep a ghutra in place on Khalif's head. It is traditionally made of goat hair. It is usually worn in the Arabian Peninsula, Iraq, Syria, southwestern Iran by Ahwazi Arabs and the Hola people, as well as in the Levant and parts of Yemen. I don't know if it's true, but some claim that it was used at night to bound a camel's legs. This prevented it from wandering off into the night". Ricky discussed his doubts about a passage through the center of the earth. The molten core would melt any foreign object, and the pressure alone would prevent any person or object from travelling on through. Scotch could see his point, but with irritation in his voice, he didn't have any answers. Towards the end of the day, Scotch proposed one more idea to his friend. He had passed the local airport several times this past week with his mother in the Subaru. There was an airplane that hasn't moved in quite a while. The idea came up to steal it on Sunday night, that would be their free ride to North Dakota. They could be back by Monday morning, just in time for school. Ricky refused to participate. It was time to hop on his bicycle and head home. On his way home, he decided to pass the airport. It wasn't far out of the way. He saw a row of old Pipers and Warriors up against the chain link fence. He remembered going on a demonstration ride with one of his uncles several years ago. Those planes don't look like much, but they are worth hundreds of thousands of dollars. A thief would most likely get caught, and he would be in big fat trouble for sure. *No thank you Scotch. You are on your own, buddy!*

TEN

ROAD TRIP TO
NORTH DAKOTA

THAT SATURDAY NIGHT, SCOTCH CALLED the local bus station. The home phone seemed to be working fine again. His ears were connected to a recording that stated the office would be open during normal operating hours on Monday the 21st. *Uh-oh, Ricky was right, closed on Sundays.* He dialed Aunt Dina's phone number again, still no answer. He was sure that he had more than enough money in the garage to solve the mortgage problem, but the authorities probably would not let a 14-year-old pay off the financial lapse without an adult being present. Besides, this found treasure is probably the government's money. They would start digging for answers after the red flag showed itself. No, he had to get this letter to his mom. He wasn't sure what day she decided on returning home. He thought about the airport idea again. It seemed like the only answer. It would be nice if he had Ricky's help, but it wouldn't be impossible on his own.

He finished all his chores on Sunday, including the return of Mrs. Ricker's ladder, all cleaned up. He knocked on the door, but nobody was home. He rewrapped the aluminum ladder and slid it back under her porch. That afternoon, he packed a bag for his long journey. This included his military ID and lanyard, Dad's unused Army parachute, a strong flashlight that Steph left down at the firepit, some cash, a lighter and a rolled-up baggie with several good-sized joints from Friday night. He remembered where Aunt Dina lived from previous visits. Scotch and his mom visited North Dakota during the summer before his dad passed away. Scotch did lots of thinking of the details of this long endeavor over the past few days. He wanted to cover all the bases. He almost forgot something before he left, the Ex-Lax from Mom's vanity. He locked the house up, put on the front light, and made his way out of the garage on his trustworthy bicycle. He closed the garage using his remote opener over his back shoulder, as he glided down the driveway. There was a coffee shop on the way called Joe and the Beanstalk. The airport up the street was smaller than MSP airport, but the runway was more than a mile and a half long. A quiet little airport, perfect for the mission. He figured on arriving at Aunt Dina's, later that night, that's if everything went well.

He purchased one of the Fall Special – Pumpkin Latte's at the coffee shop, then continued on his way. As he approached the airport perimeter, there it was, behind the eight-foot chain link fence. The barbed wire coiled around the top looked intimidating. The chariot of choice for the night was a Boeing 747-400. It was a freighter that has been parked there for a few weeks. It must have been getting some maintenance done on it. At least all the engine cowlings were buttoned up on it, unlike the last time he saw it while running errands with his mom. The wing navigation lights were on, and the main entry door was open at the top of the airstairs. *Awesome, she's powered up and the aircraft door is open for access.* The jet looked in decent shape, it was painted all white. There was a small, stenciled insignia on the side by the door. It read 'Cogan Air Cargo'. Scotch did some research' on the Company ahead of time. It was a small cargo operator out of Germany. They operated 12 B-747's. This one happened to end up in the States for now. It was probably being repaired to haul freight again utilizing a local maintenance contractor.

He threw his slim parachute pack over the fence, the section closest to the behemoth of an aircraft. Something that big would have to take off empty, with only an hour or two of fuel on board, no cargo, and a minimum crew. He ran across the airport perimeter road with his bike and hid it in the thick brush. The walk to the FBO (Fixed Base Operator) wasn't too far. All he had on his possession was his small backpack with his bare necessities. He entered the building surrounded by a security fence and walked into the lobby. The only person present was the old lady behind the desk. She looked like the secretary. Scotch played the smooth talking 14-year-old who wanted to be a pilot someday. "How are you doing today mam"? She replied, "I'm fine, but it's been a long day. Can't wait to get home and kick my feet up on the couch". "You guys stay open late"? "Well, it's not by choice. We have a couple of big wigs coming in over the next couple of hours. After the ground crew puts their planes to bed for the night, we will be closing". Scotch placed the frozen frappe on her counter. "I brought this for you, it was two for one at Joe and the Beanstalk, I already drank mine". Her face lit up, "Why bless your soul! I love that place! Make yourself at home, I just made some fresh popcorn, grab a bag and a chair". "Thanks, I just dropped by to maybe see some airplanes land. I want to be a pilot when I get older". She said, "I don't know if you'll see too much, it's starting to get dark. Josh, our head flight instructor might be back shortly. He's on a long cross-country flight with his student. He'd love to talk to a potential flight student. Things have been a little slow around here. Make yourself comfortable. Thanks again for the treat"!

Scotch plopped down on the sofa and thumbed through several old aviation magazines. There wasn't much activity in the FBO. Other than a couple of phone calls to the front desk, there was only one small airplane flying around the pattern. He occasionally glanced over to the front desk. The Ex-Lax was beginning to work. The old lady was shifting in her seat. By the sound of her straw, she just finished the last of her giant frothy drink, laced with the stool laxative. A few minutes later, she slid her headset from her large head of silver-gray hair. She disappeared down the hallway. Here was his chance. He put his official ID around his neck, grabbed his backpack and left out the security door leading to the ramp. No one was around, however a faded green golf cart with dirty white seats was outside on the ramp. It was plugged into the charger. The jet was several football fields away. He unplugged the heavy cord, threw his backpack on the passenger seat, and pressed on the pedal to get her up to max speed. The wind felt good in his long flowing hair.

He pulled up to the wingtip of the giant machine, seeing that his parachute pack was still sitting nearby in the tall grass. He let it continue to rest. There was a gray pickup parked at the edge of the ramp. It was getting dark quickly now. He made his way up the stairs to the open door. The main deck of the freighter was empty. He climbed the ladder to the connecting entryway into the upper deck. Upon opening the door, he startled a mechanic, who dropped his pen. "Who are you, and who let you up here"? Scotch thought quickly, "Hi, I'm David. I'm supposed to be meeting my dad up here in the next hour, I came out on my bicycle a little early. Dad's a pilot with Cogan. We're supposed to be doing some sort of engine runup tonight, I guess the plane's almost ready to go back to work". The sweaty mechanic replied, "Well, I know that. Me, myself, and I have been getting her ready the last couple of weeks. We're just about there, just some small items left. I just didn't think we were running her up for another few days. I'm still working on a couple of the cargo rollers down on the main deck". Scotch replied, "I guess headquarters is the boss, they're trying to rush her out of here. Every day the plane sits, they're losing out on revenue freight". Max answered back, "Go figure, money is always the bottom line around here. I assume that I need to be onboard for this engine run?". "Yes, myself, Dad, and you. It shouldn't take that long". "Well kid, I'll tell you what. If I have time, I'd like to run home quick. I need to let the wife know that I'm working late and grab a sandwich to go for the road. I'll be back in less than an hour. Don't start without me". "My Dad will probably be longer than that. Don't worry, we'll wait until you get back. I'm just going to finish some of my homework for Monday". "Alright, don't touch anything, I'll be back in a jiffy". Max closed the curtain to the cockpit and grabbed his tool bag. The boy perched himself in one of the first-class cabin seats. Scotch could hear the mechanic tromp down the ladder to the main deck, and then down the airstairs outside of the airplane, fading off into the darkness. The old jalopy of a pickup was the man's transportation out to the main gate.

Scotch knew he had little time. As it was, the old lady behind the desk was probably wondering where he went. Maybe she saw that he looked kind of bored sitting there for over twenty minutes, not much going on. *That was about to change!* He whipped the curtain open and jumped into the captain's seat. He looked around, looked at the overhead panel and scoped out the fuel situation. Alright, 73,000 pounds of fuel onboard, enough for over a couple of hours of flying. He was elated to see that all the switches and dials were just like his computer simulator at home. He was glad that his mom let him get the more advanced software version. The aircraft's electrical system was being powered by the GPU (ground power unit) located down below the nose of the plane. Next task on the venue, start the onboard APU (auxiliary power unit), so that he could disconnect the GPU down below.

This would continue to power the electrics, along with supplying bleed air pressure to start the engines. He placed the battery switch on, brought up the status displays on the primary computer screen, and cranked up the APU. Nice, it started normally and is up to speed. He transferred all electrical power to the APU and turned on some air conditioning to the cockpit now that the turbine engine out on the tail was supplying bleed air. Now for the most important part, the programming of the performance and the weight and balance. The young pilot-to-be practiced this many times on his computer, up in his bedroom. Filling in all the required boxes was the key; enter the empty weight of the airplane, fuel load, current weather parameters, departure and destination airports, routing, altitude etc. The center console's printer came to life. The results were torn off and examined. Looks like flaps 20, reduced power and still, plenty of runway to spare. The hydraulic system was powered up and the parking brake set. Now he could remove the tire chocks without having the jet possibly roll away. The ramp might appear level, but with the size and weight of an aircraft like this, one degree of incline could trigger the airplane to start rolling. Mr. Lake explained this to the boy when his father brought him to the MSP Airport. He quickly made his way down the stairs to the tarmac below. The airstairs would have to be removed out of the way so that he could taxi the giant aircraft away from its resting spot. He hand-cranked the four anchor legs on the airstairs a few inches above the ramp. He got on the back side and pushed with all his might. Once he got it rolling, momentum would take over, just like the wagon with the treasure chest. The twenty-foot-high stairs moved about two feet before getting stuck on a crack in the ramp. He really wished that Ricky was here right about now. It wasn't going to move any further. *Damn it!* Scotch came up with another idea. In the meantime, he ran to the main gear and removed the chocks. He finished up with the nose chocks, and then disconnected the large GPU. That machine was for sure, too heavy to move. After shutting down the noisy GPU, he dragged the large wooden chocks towards the grass. He retrieved his dad's black parachute and climbed up onto the nose wheel of the jet. The electronics bay access door was next. Over his head, he unlatched the release button and rotated the handle to allow the door to swing down from its hinge. He crawled up into the compartment, and closed the hatch tightly behind him, holding Steph's halogen flashlight with his mouth, the faint smell of her provocative perfume still present. He climbed the ladder to the main deck and closed that hatch. Next, he closed the main entryway door to the outdoors, and locked it tightly. The plane could now be pressurized, although his planned flight to North Dakota was not going to be at that high of an altitude. He climbed the ladder to the upper deck, and then closed that door. Now he was ready to go flying!

He jumped into the captain's seat and put the supplied headset on that was hanging up on the window post. There was the anticipated checklist waiting for him, this would assure that he didn't miss any crucial steps. Scotch checked the doors display on the main screen, making sure all the doors of the plane were closed and latched properly. Next, he placed all the fuel pumps on. He learned many of the basics over the years with the wise guidance of his dad. The rotating beacon came on for engine start or while the plane was under tow by a "Super Tug", the navigation lights stayed on anytime the electrical system was powered. A taxi light was used to see the darkened taxiways from the cockpit, far above, the landing lights were for takeoff and landing. The strobe lights came on when the airplane was about to get airborne with a clearance for take-off. Next, the air conditioning supply was turned off, to supply max bleed air from the APU, to safely start the huge engines. The GE Powerplants were started one at a time, even though the checklist allowed two at a time. No sense in rushing the whole thing, although he was running out of time. Max the mechanic would return soon. Within two minutes, the engines were all fired up and stabilized. The brake was released…. *oh crap*, the nervous boy almost forgot. He slowly opened the reverse thrusters at idle, and the jet began to roll backwards away from the GPU and the Stinar Airstairs (made right there in St. Paul, MN). After about one hundred feet, he knew the wing tips would clear all obstacles, mainly the stairs when he made the turn out of the ramp area and on to the active taxiway. He applied the brake carefully, so as not to allow the empty airplane to sit on its tail. After all, he only weighed about 450,00 pounds tonight, not the normal 872,000 pounds when fully loaded. With the parking brake set, it was time to make the professional radio call to the tower, his last obstacle to freedom.

Pilot: Tower, this is maintenance one, we're the 747 on the east ramp. We need to taxi to the west end for some engine runups. We'd like to face to the east once we get there, up against the engine blast barriers.

Tower: Roger that maintenance one. I have a couple of corporate planes inbound to land in about 30 minutes, how long will you be?

Pilot: This will take about ten minutes, then we'll be out of your way. We'll only be running them up to just a little bit more than idle power tonight.

Tower: Roger that, don't mean to rush you, but the inbound Hawkers will be landing to the west for noise abatement. They'll be exiting the runway at your location; don't think they'll be able to get around you.

Pilot: No problem, we'll call you when we're done for the taxi back to the east ramp.

Tower: Okay, maintenance one, taxi to the west ramp via taxiway Charlie and Alpha. Call the tower when you're ready to return to the ramp. Altimeter setting, 30.12.

Pilot: Maintenance one copies, we'll taxi via Charlie and Alpha, 30.12 on the meter.

Scotch released the parking brake and began his turn out of the east ramp. It didn't take much power as light as he was. He flipped his taxi lights on and began the long slow taxi down Alpha, to the other end.

Joe, the Tower operator that night, was giving most of his focus to the Twins game, live on the television. They were playing a home game against the Boston Red Sox, trying to secure the AL Central for the season. The weather was perfect on that early Fall night. Joe had his headset on one ear to monitor the radio for inbounds. It was a required job of his to monitor the radar scope, however, watching the TV stole most of his attention in the control tower. Scotch reached the other end of the field, engines all warmed up and ready to go. He switched off all the lights, even the navigation lights. Most important, he turned off his transponder, placing him in a stealth mode from being tracked on radar while enroute to North Dakota. He taxied onto runway 09, straightened out and began the power up of the powerful engines. The book says that each of the four engines produces 46,500 pounds of thrust per engine. He wouldn't need all of that tonight, even with a short runway. His performance data provided him with safety margins for the climb out. The airplane came to life! He released the brakes and started to accelerate down the runway. Joe's subliminal mind could hear the engines through his soundproof glass of the tower, but he wrote it off as being the engine runup requested by the Cogan Cargo maintenance crew. The monster of a jet with all of its lights off, got up to the required speed and rotated into the darkness. A sharp right turn, and Scotch was on his way to the well-planned navigation path. He climbed rapidly to 700 feet and leveled out using the autopilot. Using the heading bug, he turned to the south, and followed I-35 to Faribault. From there, he headed northwest to the St. Cloud Airport. After that, it was I-94 to Bismarck, then he would climb to a higher altitude, for the arrival into the Minot Airport. With the ATC 'distraction maneuver' to Faribault, the trip would be a little over 600 miles. The low altitude would keep him under the radar coverage most of the way and the 700-foot AGL altitude would be high enough to avoid hitting any cellphone and radio antennas, with the stipulation that he stayed over the interstates. His radio altimeter would track his altitude above the slowly rising terrain to the west. He would have to keep a slight climb going on his barometric altimeter. *Roughly one hour of flight time happily beats the 10-hour ride on the back of a bus!*

As Max arrived out to the ramp after the old lady opened the gate for him, he couldn't believe what he was seeing. The 747 was gone! *What the f***!* He swung the gray truck around, thrusting gravel everywhere. He raced towards the base of the tower, realizing he was in a shitload of trouble. The desperate run to the intercom system hanging on the exterior wall, reminded Max of how out of shape he was. His trembling hand pounded the buzzer several times.

> **Tower:** Hello, may I help you?

> **Mechanic:** Hey, I'm a contractor with Sparky's Elite, I've been working on the 747 the last couple of weeks. I think someone just stole it.

> **Tower:** Was Cogan expecting a repossession of the aircraft?

Mechanic: I have no idea, I just know that it's gone missing, and I am responsible for it.

Tower: Calm down sir, do you have your ID badge on you?

Mechanic: Of course, I do! I need your help!

Tower: Alright, I'm buzzing you up, take the elevator up to 9A, see you in a few.

Joe assumed with humor that the mechanic was uninformed of the engine runup down on the far end of the field. He didn't mind having a visitor tonight, it would break up the monotony. He reached for his black binoculars hanging on the wall. He looked towards the west end, where the sun disappeared below the horizon about an hour ago. There was just a hint of light from the dusk. The West Ramp was empty! He quickly gazed at his radar scope as a low flying aircraft was just disappearing to the south at 700 feet above the ground, towards Faribault.

Joe turned off the television and reached for the red phone to the Pentagon. This was some serious shit. After alerting the FAA authorities, he pulled the radar scope tapes for the last hour, and confirmed a faint trajectory towards the south, shortly after the plane departed. This information would help the appropriate agencies for the tracking projection, possibly involving a US military intercept. When Max arrived, he assured Joe that there was about 2-3 hours of fuel on board, depending on the cruising altitude. "They must be headed towards Mexico"! Max exclaimed. "They'll need to make a fuel stop on the way, maybe somewhere in Texas". Joe replied, "Calm down Max, the authorities will arrive shortly. Between all the government entities about to get involved, they'll figure this whole thing out. Homeland Security trains for this sort of thing"! Joe suggested to Max that at this time, it would be a good idea to call the Cogan Cargo office. They might as well be included in the loop.

Meanwhile, everything was going smoothly in the cockpit. The autopilot was holding course and altitude. Scotch could see the lines of taillights and headlights on I-94 below. The aircraft was humming along at 420 knots. He reached down into his sock and pulled out one of the marijuana joints that Steph left behind on Friday. He never understood why she went home to get more weed. *She must have really wanted to impress me*, he thought. Oh well, he'll find out the whole story of her early departure this upcoming week at school. For now, he placed the joint between his lips and lit it up with his lighter. The cockpit filled with a gray haze; his mind was starting to relax. He was already halfway to his destination. He extinguished the joint after a few good hits and set the roach on the center pedestal. It was time to prepare for the approach into Minot AFB. There was over 13,000 feet of runway and it had a field elevation of 1600 feet. There was an Instrument Landing System on Runway 30, the active runway. This would be an Autoland using the sophisticated capability of the autopilot system. Scotch picked the military base to avoid disrupting the passenger travel over at Minot International. *Maybe he would be in less trouble if he ever got caught.* He would get the plane all set up after a climb to 5000 feet. The airplane would be all configured to intercept the glide slope, then follow it down and land. The plane would even come to a full stop after a picture-perfect landing with the engines powering back to idle as it decelerated down the runway, using only the autopilot. The captain normally takes over from there and taxis into the ramp. Tonight, it would remain on the centerline somewhere at the far end of the runway at idle power with brake pressure holding it to a stop; nobody would be onboard.

Back in St. Paul, the Dakota County officials along with the St. Paul and Eagan Police Department swarmed the small airfield at the south end of town. Their objective was to obtain security surveillance equipment in and around the main entrance. What they found was quite a surprise. There were two corporate jets on the ramp, and the passengers were wandering around the FBO. After a brief search of the building, they found an old lady in the women's restroom. Her head had been twisted 270 degrees. Her bloodied body slumped over the toilet with no one else around. In the corner of the stall, there rested a pair of what looked like oversized clown shoes. They were fabricated out of bright yellow vinyl material. They had a strong aroma of fresh strawberries. Beside them was a large clutch of helium balloons pressed against the ceiling of the restroom, their strings hanging down like colorful spaghetti. There was at least a dozen of them. The policemen on the scene only found three security cameras. The cassettes had been removed, and all the cameras had the scent of strawberries. The passengers from the Hawker Jets were confused at this point. They were counting on transportation and hotel accommodations to be waiting for them.

Scotch climbed the jet to 5000 feet. It was time for the approach into MIB (Minot AFB). He was thirty miles from the destination field.

> **Pilot:** Minot Tower, this is Cheyenne 4962B, 30 miles southeast of the field, we're inbound for the ILS to 30.

> **Tower:** Cheyenne 4962B, will this be a full stop?

> **Pilot:** That's affirmative, we have the current weather, we'll be parking on the south side.

> **Tower:** I don't have you on radar yet, how many miles out did you say?

Pilot: Currently 27 miles out, we have the field in sight.

Tower: Okay 62B, you are cleared for the visual to 30, call me on a 5-mile final.

Pilot: Roger that, 4962B is cleared to land on 30, we'll call you on a 5-mile final.

Scotch unbuckled from his seat, grabbed his bag and his parachute. The autopilot had captured the localizer for lateral left and right guidance, and just as he was leaving the cockpit through the flimsy curtain, he looked back to see that the auto throttles were powering back as it captured the glideslope. Scotch jumped back into the seat. He almost forgot a couple of things. *Configuration*! He extended out all the flaps and dropped the landing gear. Next, he shut down the number two engine, the one closest to the main cabin door. He wasn't sure if this was necessary, but the thought of his chute getting sucked into that engine after he exited, was a scary image in his mind. His body would be shredded by the turbine engine, or he would get lucky and fall to his death far below. For the remaining task, he reached up on the overhead panel, and switched all the exterior lights on – the navigation lights, the strobes, the rotating beacons and of course, all the landing lights. He turned off all the bleed air supply, this would fully depressurize the slightly pressurized aircraft, allowing him to be able to open the cabin door. The aircraft was now fully stabilized, he ran for the ladder. Once he jumped onto the main deck, he quickly strapped into the parachute, his backpack in hand. He cranked open the large handle of the main entryway and pulled the door inwards, then pushing it back out until it locked in the open position.

Tower: 4962B, how many miles are you showing now?..........4962B, do you read Minot Tower?

"Uh-oh Bob, I've got a Cheyenne on short final, and I lost communication with him. I show no record of a PPR (Prior Permission Required), and he is hauling ass"! Troy held his binoculars up towards final approach. It was still dusk in ND. "That is no Cheyenne! That's a large Transport Jet, and I never cleared him to land"! He grabbed for the red phone. Something wasn't right. Bob grabbed the black phone at another desk in the tower and alerted all military personnel to the landing end of runway 30. The Pentagon put two and two together, this was the missing airplane!

Scotch tightened his straps and did a pencil dive straight down, a required maneuver to avoid getting hit by the left wing, or even worse, the number one engine that was still running. A strap on his parachute pack got hooked on the hinge of the door. Scotch suddenly found himself being body slammed into the exterior of the doorframe. The noise of the slipstream was intense, and the air was very cold. Soon, he would be too low to successfully parachute. Or worse, upon landing, he could fall from his 26-foot position and then get run over by the jets large wheels as it decelerated down the runway. He pulled his knees up into a tuck position and pushed off the fuselage as hard as he could. It was over before he knew it. As things got quieter and the plane raced away from him, he pulled the main chord. The expensive low altitude chute that his dad acquired from the Army, worked perfectly. Now his job was to aim for the highway several thousand feet below, so as not to get caught up in the tall trees aligning the interstate. As he came within touchdown distance, he rapidly steered the black canopy to the edge of the woods. Bam, he was down. He hit hard, but he was okay. The chute draped over his body as it deflated in an instant. Scotch laid there quietly, listening for signs of any passing motorists stopping out on Route 2 – nothing out of the norm, they kept driving by. He crawled to the edge of the chute and peeked outside. Several cars were driving away from him, no brake lights in sight. He sprung to his feet, balled up the chute and disappeared into the woods. One more look back towards the highway, still nothing suspicious. *Oh my God, I made it!* As he was making his way along a worn path, he noticed a ballfield that was well lit up ahead. There was a high school football game going on. It was the Minot Magicians Varsity Football Team. He knew right where he was. Aunt Dina's house was just on the other side of the high school. He paused to smoke the last of the joint that he slid back into his sock, while letting his body recuperate. The pulse of his heart was beating like a piston at full throttle. Next to him in the woods was an old, abandoned fire pit. He knew just what had to be done. The balled-up parachute fit perfectly in the middle of the pit. A small flame flicked from his lighter. He lit the canopy in several places and the flame instantly engulfed the whole chute. It was initially very bright, but he was far enough back in the woods where none of the spectators under the stadium lights would notice. Suddenly the crowd roared with cheers. When Scotch peeked through the bushes, a player was running as fast as he good towards the goal posts. Touchdown! Perfect timing for a distraction, it was like magic! He finished the joint and began the trek across the high school grounds. The smell of popcorn, hotdogs and brats filled the evening air. Scotch had the munchies.

Meanwhile, not far away, the large jet flared perfectly and touched down softly. The autobrakes engaged and the aircraft slowly decelerated to the far end of the field. There were dozens of blue and red flashing lights, some still racing towards the runway.

The Pentagon Official in charge: General Jackson, are you there!

Army General: Yes sir, I am being approached by the 747, I am clear of the runway! Everything looks normal...normal deceleration, on the centerline, engines at idle!

Pentagon Official: I want you to arrest every bastard on board! There may be hostages as well! Treat everyone as a suspect! I repeat, take everyone into custody!

Army General: Yes Sir, we're on it, my men are surrounding the aircraft as we speak. I'll report back after the apprehension!

Twenty minutes later.

Army General: Hello, this is General Jackson again. Sir, we have completed the search of the aircraft after fully securing the area as well as powering down the jet. There was nobody on board sir.

Pentagon Official: What the hell are you talking about. Who flew the goddamn plane?

Army General: I know sir, we're looking into it.... full investigation sir.

ELEVEN

RETURN HOME TO EAGAN

SCOTCH FINALLY MADE HIS WAY to the driveway of Aunt Dina's. As he approached the lighted front porch, he could see his mom and Aunt Dina in a couple of fancy straight back armchairs through the pale-yellow curtains. One of the windows was open. They were facing each other and carrying on a conversation in the formal dining room. The kaleidoscope colors of the Tiffany Lamp were stunning. There was jazz music playing in the background. He rang the doorbell. Scotch heard Aunt Dina place her drink onto the table. She then verified that her nightgown wasn't showing too much cleavage and headed to the front door.

"Scotch! What the hell are doing here?" Cheryl ran to the door quickly to see if it was really her son. Both women were shocked. Cheryl asked, "Scotch, is everything alright"? Her son replied, "Well if you invite me in, I'll tell you what it's all about". They stepped back; Aunt Dina opened the door all the way. Scotch proceeded to the table and slid his backpack from his shoulders. He unzipped the bag and presented his mom with the letter. She grabbed it from his hands and read the labelling on the front of the letter. She noticed that it was addressed to 'Current Resident'. The street address was that of the neighbor, Annelle Ricker. Without saying a word, she removed the letter from the opened envelope. Aunt Dina invited her nephew into the kitchen to have something to eat. As the two of them left the room, Cheryl read the letter in its entirety. She took a deep breath and joined the two chatty ones in the kitchen. "Oh son, this letter isn't meant for us, I believe it is Mrs. Ricker's. Your Dad and I paid our mortgage off last year with your grandparent's Trust Fund. How could you make such a silly mistake"? "Mom, let me see the envelope"! He examined the front, and clearly saw that it wasn't their address. Scotch suddenly felt small and immature. "I'm a freaking idiot! I am so sorry". "Don't worry about it Scott, it's great to see that you've come to visit. Did you get a round trip bus ticket, or what"? "No mom, it was a one-way". His mom laughed, "Well I was planning on heading back tomorrow. Besides, we need to get you back for school. I'll get us a couple of bus tickets tomorrow, looks like you'll miss one day at school. I'll have to call the office in the morning to explain, don't let me forget". The rest of the night was spent catching up with his aunt. The women let Scotch have a couple of adult beverages. There was plenty of food, and the music was cool. Scotch retired to bed before the ladies did, it had been a long night for him. Aunt Dina showed him to Sheila's abandoned bedroom. The room was painted light purple and the four-posted bed was adorned with a white lacy comforter. The dresser and bureau were neatly topped with statues, fake flower arrangements and some cheap jewelry. Dina spoke up, "Scotch, I hope this will do you for a night. The sheets are clean, and you can open the windows if it gets too warm in here. Sheila would be happy to know that her cousin was sleeping in her bed tonight, I bet she misses it"! Scotch asked his aunt, "Why does she have so many stuffed animals everywhere, it must be a pain to make up the bed in the morning"? "Oh, you can just put them over on the floor there. Sheila collected them throughout her childhood. Look at this one here". She lifted an old still gray teddy bear from the pillow. His stomach had been cut wide open, and then sewed back up with a big vertical zipper scar. "His name is Stitch; it was Sheila's first attempt at becoming a mortician". The boy asked, "How old was she when she did that"? With a deep breath and a laugh, "I think she was your age". His aunt turned toward the door with a whimsical look on her face. She had a little more conversation left in her to share with her sister. Scotch drifted off to sleep quickly. Hours later, there was a scratching noise coming from the bedroom closet. He laid there for several minutes staring up at the ceiling, then he heard it again. There was no clock in the bedroom, so he didn't have a clue what time it was. It must be an animal in the wall, or in the closet. He needed to go to the bathroom, it would probably be safe. He pulled back the sheet, sat up and swung his legs over the side of the bed. He jumped down from the tall bed with a thud and made his way to the bedroom door. As he grabbed the brass handle and opened the door, he realized that it was the closet door. Someone on the other side of the door pushed it opened with a lot of force, knocking the boy on his ass. He looked up in the darkness and was knocked over the head with a heavy object. When he came to, he was lying back in Sheila's bed with his arms and legs tied to the four bedposts. His mouth was full of a rolled-up ball of cloth held in place with several strands of sticky tape. He tried his best to scream for help, but it was useless. His cheek skin stretched beneath the tape. Next, an overhead spotlight was switched on. Scotch could make out a silhouette of a large man with a fuzzy body suit in the bright glare. One of his paws was clenching some type of a power tool. It was silver with a black cord coming from it. It suddenly came to life with a high RPM buzzing noise, almost like a dentist drill, but not making too much noise. He tried to thrash his way out of the ropes while trying to scream again. The thin twine wouldn't give, causing him pain to his wrists and ankles. He felt a cold disc touch his chest, it then turned into a burning feeling. The smell in the room became different. A stinging pain was ripping through his skin and the disc was bouncing off his ribs. The man in the bear suit began to quietly laugh as he applied more downward pressure on the sinister machine. Now he could hear the hardness of his bones being splintered through with the device……. then…all was quiet and the bright light went out. As he lay there in shock for several minutes, he could see through the bottom of the window shade that the sky was slowly getting lit outside. Yes, it was the sunrise beginning to take shape. Then a door handle could be heard slowly rotating and the bedroom light came on. His mother peeked her head in and said, "Come on sleepy head, time to get up. Aunt Dina is making us a nice country breakfast". She opened the door all the way and made her way to the bedside. She bent over and picked an object off the floor. It was Sheila's teddy bear named Stitch. She placed it on the end of the bed and pulled the vinyl shade down a couple of inches and then lifted it to the top of the window. The sun was just beginning to rise above the treetops. "I got us 10:00 tickets, Aunt Dina is going to drive us to the station after breakfast. I'll see you in the kitchen". She turned and left the room. Scotch felt his chest for blood or an open wound, nothing. That was the most realistic nightmare that he could remember. He realized that his arms and legs were free again. With his left foot, he kicked the gray bear back onto the floor. He jumped to his feet and got dressed. Before he left the room, he peeked in the closet. There was an old grinding tool lying in a carpenter's canvas tote bag. He shut the door and headed down to breakfast. On the way, he took a well needed pitstop at the bathroom. The breakfast was wonderful. There were fried eggs, sausage links, home fries and English muffins. The coffee was freshly brewed, and the orange juice was hand squeezed. The three of them had a mellow conversation, mostly about the local area, work and the likelihood of Scotch and his mom coming back to visit in the summer for a couple of weeks. As always, Aunt Dina asked about Scotch's future endeavors and career desires. "I think I want to be a pilot when I grow up". He gave the same answer as a couple of years ago.

While Aunt Dina cleaned up the kitchen, Cheryl called the bus company again, querying about upgrading to the First-Class section in the front of the bus. She gave the man her credit card information and hung up the phone when the conversation was over. "That will give us a little more leg room"! Scotch was not looking forward to the long bus ride, but it would give him time to think about things. There were some loose ends back at home that he needed to fix. He needed to help the Rickers, especially Amy. How could he mastermind the gift of $30,000 to the family next door, without raising eyebrows when the law officers showed up at the Ricker's residence on Wednesday.

Twenty minutes into the bus ride, he smelt a strong odor of whiskey. He thought his mother was sound asleep next to him, but when he looked over at her, it all made sense. A long white straw was protruding from her blue wind breaker, leading up to her lips. Her face was hidden within her hood, only her dark sunglasses protruding. He decided to let it go unnoticed, being that they were surrounded by nuns from a Minneapolis congregation. Now would be a good time to finish up his homework for Tuesday. The bus driver made several stops at some rest areas, it felt good to stretch the legs. At the last one, there was a dark green truck for sale. It almost looked like a used military vehicle. That's it! Scotch thought about the behemoth of the military truck in the Ricker's driveway. He will purchase it for $30,000 and leave it stored in the neighbor's driveway. Maybe someday, he could get it running again, then fix it up to its original condition. He pulled out a piece of paper and started to write up a Bill of Sale to the Ricker Family. Now, he just had to figure out how to change some of the treasured loot to cold hard cash. The old man at the coin shop came to mind first. The rest of the bus ride went fast after he devised his plan. The bus pulled into the Eagan bus depot in the middle of the afternoon. Ten minutes later, they pulled into their driveway in a green and white cab that said SUBURBAN on the side. The first thing that they noticed was an orange dump truck parked in front of their house. It had the dormant yellow rotating beacons on top of the cab. Attached to the rear of the truck was a long trailer with a backhoe parked on its bed. The door of the truck was labelled "Eagan Parks Department". There was not a worker around. There was also a horse trailer parked in front of the truck, but it was empty. Scotch thought that it was too small to house a normal size horse, let alone a full-grown buffalo! "What do we have here", his mom said with a quirky smile. As Scotch exited the car, he noticed tire tracks on their side lawn from a heavy piece of equipment, maybe the backhoe. They led down back to the woods. Suddenly, he had a lump in his throat and all his energy left his body. His Mom carried their things through the garage. "Mom, I'm going to check out the woods down back, see what they did". Cheryl replied, "Alright, be careful. I'm going to unpack the bags and start dinner. Don't stay out there for too long". "I won't"!

As he made his way down the path, he confirmed that the tire marks were from the loader. At one point in the path where it got narrow, the driver of the machine took a direct route to the cave. Scotch followed the newly made path that would be temporary in nature. The cave was gone! The earth had been smoothed over with no evidence of a break in the surface. The smell of dirt filled his nostrils. The yellow crime tape was gone. *Was Kalif and his team buried alive? Was the cave explored by city officials?* He had no answers. He thought about the treasure in his garage. He ran up the path to the back porch. His Mom was sitting at the patio table with a glass of bourbon and a half-burned cigarette in one hand, the long gray ash getting ready to fall onto the table. She was focused on an article in the newspaper. "Scotch, there was a plane stolen from the airport up the street". "Really"? "Yah, it says that it was a cargo plane. Possible suspects are involved with a drug lord from Central America. They found it abandoned somewhere out in the Midwest. Damn drugs and crime are taking over the world"! "Mom, my homework is done, I think I'm going to fish the pond for a little bit". "Supper is going to be ready in about twenty-five minutes, you better make it fast"! Scotch went into the garage to retrieve his rod and reel. He saw the canvas pile in the corner, covering up the treasure chest. What a relief, it was just as he had left it. He grabbed his pole and headed down back. Something red caught his eye down by the pond. It was Stephanie's small purse that she kept her weed in along with a pack of rolling papers and a half empty pack of cigarettes. There was even a lighter inside. He rolled over a rotten log that was nearby and grabbed a night crawler. He baited his hook and cast it out to the distant bank. Perfect cast he thought to himself. He wiped his hands on his jeans and revisited the red purse. In the next few minutes, he managed to roll a good size spleef and lit it up. He handled the hit much better this time, exhaling a grassy smelling plume of smoke. The smell of marijuana reminded him of a chocolate donut and coffee down at the local Mister Donut. It also kind of smelled like a skunk. He finished the joint and leaned back against the grassy bank. He looked over to Amy's house and noticed several lights on in the house. *Oh good, they must be back from their weekend trip. I'll have to pay a visit after school tomorrow. They don't know it yet, but I am about to buy the Army truck from them.* Maybe he could fix it up and take Amy to the prom in it in a couple of years, he giggled under his breath. The weed was starting to distort his rational thinking. His bobber started to jump up and down. He lazily watched it for a minute then grabbed his rod and reeled the fish in. It was only a four-inch bluegill, he was hoping for a larger one. He collected his things, hid the purse in the woodpile and headed up to the house for dinner. The baked enchiladas were going to be a big treat right about now. Scotch had the munchies. He even thought about kicking his heels up and using some of the unopened ghost pepper sauce in the cupboard.

As he lay in bed that night, he devised his plan for the trip to the coin shop. He would fill his dad's bowling bag with 180 of the gold coins. He would go to the old man at the shop and ask for enough coin holders for the coins. He would falsely claim that he had a buyer for $175 apiece. That would trump the old man's original assessment of $150 per coin. He would also have to leave for school earlier than normal in the morning to retrieve his bike out of the woods by the airport.

Later that night, Scotch got up to use the bathroom. After he flushed, he realized that he never actually looked under the gray canvas in the garage to see if anyone messed with the chest full of coins. He quietly crept down the stairs and moved swiftly into the garage. He lifted a corner of the canvas and saw that indeed, nobody disturbed the treasure. The shiny padlock that he found in the basement was still solidly fastened through the clasp. He then decided to smoke the last joint that he had in his backpack. He grabbed the lighter and snuck out onto the back porch. He left all the lights off so as not to wake his mom or the neighbors. There was enough light from the moon to see out into the backyard. Several hits later, something caught his attention from way down back. It was even beyond Billy Preston's house. It was a block of blue light floating in the air, about ten feet off the ground. He inhaled the last hit of the joint as he watched it slowly move from left to right. A raindrop was felt on his cheek. The object was no threat to him, just perked his curiosity. As he squinted his eyes, there seemed to be a group of people on some sort of floating platform. Everything was aglow with a light blue light. It was

bright enough to be able to see it from so far away. The rain began
to fall quite steadily. Lightning flashed off in the distance. The
craft stopped in midair and seemed to turn towards him. There
was a tall man in the center of the object with a group of people
hunched down on the platform. Before he could surmise what
was going on, it began to approach him rapidly. He ran to the
inside corner of the porch and crouched down, making his body
as small as possible. This shielded him from the rain as well. He
sat quietly with his arms folded around his head. When he took
a glimpse to see where this thing was headed, it was already past
the woodpile and heading right for him! He could now make out
Khalif's stern face and his long white robe. Everything appeared
light blue. There was a soft whooshing sound starting to come
into Scotch's earshot. The large platform hummed to within 10
feet of his hiding place. The sound idled down to almost nothing,
like an old steam locomotive pulling into a train station and
shutting down its engine. The floating platform looked to be
about 30 feet long and 12 feet wide. There were strange symbols
on the side, comparable to Chinese or Japanese symbols, but with
no sharp edges on the markings. The letters were more circular
with dots in certain areas. There were lights all around the craft,
but no signs of light bulbs with filaments, just opaque circles
of colored light. They were emitting the subtle light blue glow
lighting up the dark rainy forest. Khalif entered Scotch's mind
with no words, just like he always had. "Scotch, it is time to go.
You must join us and travel to the heavens of eternity. You have
proved yourself, and you are welcome to join us on this fruitful
journey". Scotch couldn't believe what he was hearing. As he
looked towards the passengers, he was starting to recognize faces.
He made out Sandy, her boyfriend Nick, Damon, Billy Preston,
Uncle Billy, and Uncle Charlie and maybe even his dad in the
back row. They, and many more were all looking down to avoid
eye contact with Scotch. An uncontrollable force shifted his head

back to center, only allowing him to focus on Khalif. "It is time to leave everything behind, all your wants, needs and desires. These are all useless to you now. Come with us, come into the eternal heavens! You will not be disappointed"! Scotch was not believing that any of this was real. "This is very real son. I don't know if I can give you this opportunity again. We are all done here, we are being called to return. You will lose one more evil person in your life, this will be a sign to you that my proposal is real. I was sent by your father to protect you and your mother. I accelerated your maturity as a young adult, exposed you to every phobia imaginable, you are now ready". Scotch felt totally drained. His body was signaling him to just give in. His heart was saying, *no, this is the work of the devil!* With all his might and energy, he looked directly into Khalif's eyes. Even further than that, he was looking into the man's soul. "I am not ready to leave the Earth. I have too much to do still. I must take care of my loved ones and complete my journey called LIFE! Leave now, I am done talking to you". The passengers on the floating craft were all making painful moans. Scotch was preparing himself to be struck down with an unforgivable force at any second. Suddenly the craft began to rise. The volume of the whooshing sound increased. The nose of the ship tilted upwards and slowly accelerated skywards. The flimsy treetops parted to the side as the massive ship created some unforeseen thrust. In no time, it was out of sight. The rain ceased. One of the passengers lost a hat. Scotch went over to pick it up. It was a military beret that had a label attached to the brim. It read – Mike Chester. Scotch walked back into the house with the beret in a daze, and secured the door shut. He quietly made his way back upstairs, brushed his teeth and fell asleep. He had a lot on his plate for tomorrow.

TWELVE

BACK TO NORMAL, ALMOST

THE NEXT DAY AFTER SCHOOL, Scotch finally got caught up with all of his schoolwork after the long weekend. He raced home on his bike that he retrieved that morning from the airport, to get the coins. Previously, he counted out a portion of them and placed them on a bath towel in the bowling bag. He exchanged his book bag for a glass of fruit punch, gulped it down and left everything on the counter. Minutes later, he raced down the driveway on his bicycle. The awkward weight of the bag was causing him to lean towards one side to compensate. The bike ride was longer than usual. As he pulled up to the coin shop, the sign on the door said CLOSED. An old wrinkly white hand covered with age spots, reached behind the dusty aluminum louvers, and flipped the sign to OPEN. Just then, the commercial deadbolt made a click and the door opened. The sharp chime of the security bell rang. "Come on in young man, I saw you coming. I was just about ready to leave out the back, it's been kind of slow today. Are you ready to sell me that coin"? "No sir, I have another buyer, but I would like to buy enough of those plastic coin canisters to hold 180 of these coins". He placed his shiny coin on the counter for the old man to size it up one more time. "Did I hear you say 180 coins"? "Yep, it's all I have. My buyer is going to give me $31,500 in cash". The old man could not believe what he was hearing. "Son, do you have these coins with you"? "Yeah, they're out next to my bike". The old man flew from behind the counter and headed to the front door. "Come on kid, let's bring them in here where it's safe". The old man held open the door as Scotch returned with his bowling bag. He thought about the worth of close to $38000 if all the coins were in the same condition as the specimen that he looked at. "I'll tell you what sir, I'm kind of tired of lugging these things around with me. If you can give me $30,000 in cash, I will take your offer". "Well now, now, I can write you a check, who should I make it out to, your parents"? "No sir, I would like you to drive to your bank this afternoon and get three ½ inch stacks of $100 dollar bills. It's the only way I'm going to do this deal". "Well, alright. Meet me out back with your bicycle and throw it in the back of my truck. I have to lock the shop up and grab my briefcase. I'll see you in a minute". Scotch raced around back, there was only one truck in the sandy lot. It was a butterscotch-colored Chevy from the 70's. The windows were open, and the tailgate was down. There was a pile of sticks in the back and two white plastic bags of trash. He loaded his bike into the bed and closed the tailgate. He opened the passenger door. It sounded as if it hadn't been opened in years. It made a loud creaking noise followed by a snap when it was fully ajar. The interior was hot with the smell of melted vinyl and plastic. He closed the door with another loud creak and then a bang as it latched. He looked over at the back door of the shop and realized that the coins were with the old man. *Was this even his truck?* What if he had just been robbed? After a few moments, the gray steel door opened and the old man in the suit backed out with the empty bowling bag and his briefcase. He locked three deadbolts with his large key ring and punched in a code on the door pad. He made his way to the truck and off they went to the bank.

As they pulled into the bank, the old man took out his wallet. He opened the leather pouch and peeled away a twenty-dollar bill. "Here son, go grab us a couple of cheeseburgers with fries and a couple of cokes next door, I'll meet you back here". Scotch assumed the man was going to take care of business. He wanted this to end quickly, not wanting to get into any kind of trouble. Across the vacant parking lot next door, sat a police cruiser. Both officers were staring at the beige truck that just pulled in. Scotch recognized them immediately. It was Jake Reynolds and his partner Dave. Scotch decided to go around the other side of the bank, he didn't want any confrontation. As he popped out of the alley way and entered the burger joint, the first person that he noticed was Mitch, *the jock who had it all*. Mitch instantly recognized his classmate and came from behind the counter. He threw a dish rag down on the front counter, and rapidly approached Scotch. His right arm came from nowhere and landed a punch on Scotch's right cheek. It wasn't a solid hit. "I don't know what you're up to, but you're nothing but trouble, Scotch". The manager witnessed the whole thing from the deep fryer station. He came from behind the counter and got face to face with Mitch. "This type of non-sense will not be tolerated in my restaurant! Grab your things and get out of here! I'll mail your last paycheck to you. You're finished Mitch"! As the disgruntled worker left the restaurant, the manager consoled Scotch. Mitch looked back through the store front window with a revengeful look. The meal was prepared quickly at no charge. Scotch returned to the Chevy truck with the supersized burgers and the twenty-dollar bill. The officers were still staring at the pick-up truck. The nervous kid was ready for an ambush that would derail the whole plan. *Was this all a set-up?* Suddenly, there was the sound of a large heavy skidding vehicle, a quiet popping noise and several shrieking screams. The officer's blue lights turned on as the back tires peeled out. The sirens came on with a deafening shrill, just as the old man was returning around the corner with a very nervous look. He turned his head towards the direction of the police car, only to watch it speed away out of sight. As he climbed in the cab of the pick-up, he removed the stacks of cash from his attaché and put them in the empty bowling bag. He assured the boy that it was all there. Scotch and the old man sat in the hot pickup with the windows down and ate their meal. The commotion continued off in the distance as the sirens were increasing in numbers. The blare of an approaching ambulance and possibly fire trucks drew near. "I have your change, sir". "Oh, you can keep it. This burger is wonderful, really hits the spot". The old man replied, "I wonder what the hell is going on up the street". The boy asked the old man if he ever thought of having a co-worker at the shop. The old man (who never gave Scotch his name), explained that he never trusted anyone. Plus, there was never a rush of customers, the workload was always light. "When you get a little older, come back and see me son". At his age, his days were numbered. The boy would never get the opportunity to work at The Coin Shop. Scotch decided that he wanted to ride his bike home, it wasn't that far. The bowling bag was a lot lighter now and much more manageable. After exiting the truck and retrieving his bicycle from the back, the old man did a U-turn in the parking lot and sped away. Scotch wanted to go check out the commotion up the street in the other direction. He was greeted with a large gathering of spectators and lots of emergency vehicles. Some witnesses appeared to be in shock. A large tour bus was diagonally blocking the road. The focus of attention was a mangled bloody body wedged under the front wheel of the bus. The high-speed vehicle contacted a boy's head, smacking it to the pavement and dragging the body a short distance as it came to a halt. Scotch recognized the plaid shirt. It was Mitch. The dead body lay motionless, as the authorities tried to figure it all out. It looked as if Mitch was coming from the smoke shop across the street. He must have come from between the two parked vans, distracted by a beautiful blonde in a mini-skirt and collided with the speeding bus. She was obviously in shock, while spewing off her story to one of the detectives, tears in her eyes. That explained the popping noise before the skidding of the large tires. The impact of the boy's head left a round imprint on the front of the aluminum tour bus, just beneath the right windshield. His head split in half, and he was rapidly bleeding out onto the pavement. Scotch turned his bike away and pedaled in the other direction. He felt sick to his stomach.

When he rode up the driveway at a high speed towards the open garage, he noticed someone in the front door of the Ricker's house staring out the glass storm door. *It was Amy!* She waved and smiled. She was in her pajamas. He would have to check in with his mother and have something quick to eat with her in the kitchen. He left the bowling bag of money in the garage and went into the house. Cheryl was pouring a large handle of bourbon into a tall glass of ice. "Ahh, how was my son's day back at school"? "It was good mom. Got a book report to do on WWII military vehicles. After supper, I'd like to go next door and visit with Mrs. Ricker. I thought maybe I could get some more details from her husband's military past. He probably had lots of experience with many vehicles, including the one in his driveway". "Maybe she saved some of his old manuals and books! Don't stay out too late and tell her I said hi. Oh, and give this letter back to her, tell her it ended up in our mailbox. I taped it shut". Cheryl wondered at that point, who would be their new neighbors once the Ricker's got evicted.

Scotch wasted no time. He gobbled down his dinner, grabbed the bill of sale and the bowling bag of cash from the garage and headed next door through the hedges. As he knocked at the front door, he wondered if this was the proper door to be at. Mrs. Ricker got funny about that in the past. The front light came on, and the door slowly opened. Amy pushed the storm door towards Scotch and invited him in. She grabbed his arm and brought him down the hallway and into the living room. The house smelled like weed. There was no dog and no Mrs. Ricker. Amy had on a bright white robe, like the ones at a fancy hotel. The two of them sat on the couch. A small bong shaped like a beautiful mermaid was on the coffee table. The bowl was filled with bright green plant-like matter. Scotch could feel the invite coming. "Scotch, there is something I need to tell you". "Oh my god, I have something to tell you as well". He handed her the taped envelope that he mistakenly received in the mail. She looked at the sender's address. "Is this about our unpaid mortgage"? He replied, "Yes, I am so sorry that I opened it. It was sent to our mailbox by mistake, and I assumed it was meant for us since my dad was in the military too". "Oh dear, I received another copy yesterday as well. I don't know what to do, I am so confused"! She immediately leaned into him and started to cry. Scotch wrapped his arms around her, comforted by her familiar scent and warmth. "What does your mom think about the whole thing"? In between sobs, she took a deep breath and looked him in the eyes. "That's what I need to talk to you about. My mom had a horrific accident this past weekend. SHE'S DEAD"! "Amy, that's terrible, what happened? Why didn't you call me"? She wiped her eyes and carried on. "I was thinking that you thought that I am just some ditzy girl next door. I haven't seen you in a while and I wasn't sure if you wanted to hear my sad story". "That's crazy talk, I fell in love with you the second I laid my eyes on you. Amy, you mean the world to me! I want to get to know you better starting right now! So, tell me what happened". "Well, the day we arrived at my Uncle Henry's farmhouse in Maple, Wisconsin, my mom decided to go into the woods to harvest some Chanterelle Mushrooms. After talking with Uncle Henry for a short while, who is my mom's younger brother, mom went about her business. I was on the porch with their Black Lab Duke drinking my lemonade. My uncle was in the process of cutting down a large oak tree. It had to be three feet in diameter and over 100 feet tall. The chainsaw droned at full power as he was completing the second triangular cut. There was a large snapping noise, then the monster of a tree fell away from the house. It collided with another large oak and suddenly shifted to the right. My uncle screamed, "Annie, shit, get the hell out of there, NOW"! My mother sprung to her feet and darted to the left. She went right into the path of the falling wooden tower. There was a large thump as it hit the forest floor. I joined my uncle and ran towards my mom. I started thinking about the trauma of being a first responder and thought about having to do first aid treatment that I learned over the years. When we arrived at her location, she was under the dead center of the tree. Her sun hat and the basket of mushrooms lay next to the fallen tree, covered with a dark red blood. My mom was gruesomely crushed. It was terrible, she didn't have a chance"! She held him tight again. She was sobbing much louder now, as if demons were escaping her body. He held her shaking body as he rubbed her back. After a few minutes, she wiped her eyes. Amy reached for the bong and lethargically lit the bowl with a lighter. She inhaled from the pipe deeply and passed it to Scotch. She had a questionable, painful look in her eye. He instantly reached for the bong and joined in. The rapid gesture made her face relax; she was at peace. After each of the kids took several more hits, Amy asked "What am I going to do? I need your help honey". "Well for starters, we need to clean this place up and air it out. You are getting some very important visitors tomorrow from the State Department". "How the hell am I going to come up with that kind of money? I don't even have a job. My uncle says everything was left to me by my parents, but I don't even know what that means. Obviously, the house wasn't paid for......what else don't I know"? "Don't worry sweetie, I have us covered. Here is the plan". He pulled out the Bill of Sale. I want to buy the Army Truck in your driveway. He slid the bowling bag across the coffee table. "Go ahead, open it up". "Scotch, I don't even know what that hunk of junk is worth". She grabbed the Bill of Sale and read it over quickly. She then zipped open the bowling bag and her face lit up. "Oh my God, this can't be happening"!!! "It is my dear Amy. As of tomorrow, you are going to be the proud owner of this beautiful house"! She got off the couch rapidly, her untied robe falling around her in the process. She was wearing nothing but a pink thong and a matching silky bra. "Follow me Scotch". She grabbed his hand and headed for the top of the basement stairs. At arm's length, he could see her perfectly shaped buttocks with the thong riding deeply between her cheeks. "What about the dog Amy"? "Oh, he wasn't ours. That was Uncle Henry's neighbor's dog from Wisconsin. We brought it back to him over the weekend. Mr. Sidel had gone on a hunting trip last week, and we were just watching it for him". The dog doesn't get along with Uncle Henry's, so we took on the burden.

The two lovebirds made their way down the stairs into the dimly lit basement. It was incredibly clean. There was a large queen-sized bed in the center of the room. The lighting in the room looked more like a dance hall. The bed was folded back with satin sheets, lots of matching pillows and a satin comforter off to one side. Amy flipped the stereo on softly as it played a romantic tune from the early eighties. As he was undressing, she lit some candles on the nightstand. The two of them met in the middle of the bed and made out like passionate lovers. All the stress and fears subsided. Hours later, Scotch awoke in the dimly lit room. He rolled towards Amy as if he was dreaming the whole thing. Her beautiful eyes met his gaze from inches away. They began to kiss, with their tongues exploring each other's mouths. They held each as if never wanting to release. Scotch pulled back. "Amy, I have to get back home. My mom will be wondering where I am, tomorrow is a school day. Are you ready to work out the mortgage with the authorities tomorrow"? "I am more than ready, after a little bit of cleaning up. Will you come over and see me after school tomorrow"? "Of course, but I am worried about you not having a lawyer or any adult present for that matter when you meet with these people tomorrow". They both made their way up to the kitchen. "Amy, should I get my mom involved? I can fill her in on the whole story tonight. Maybe she can come over and help you tomorrow". Amy turned to Scotch, put her arms around his waist, and pulled him in close. "Scotch, I talked this over with my Uncle Henry. I should have told this to you before, but I am 19 years old. When I turned 18, I was fully emancipated in the State of Minnesota. I therefore can own a house, as well as own and operate a motor vehicle, such as Mom's Cadillac that I drove home from Wisconsin. And the question about your mother getting involved, that would be a big NO! I am totally in love with you, and I don't want to ruin what we have. I want to be your secret lover until you turn 18. Then I will convince you to marry me". She had the most beautiful smile that Scotch had ever seen. The blood was rushing to his head. His whole future was being created right before his eyes.

That night, he arrived back home to find his mom sleeping in the den. It appeared that she decided to start smoking in the house. An old ashtray from the garage was sitting on the end table next to an empty glass. She was sound asleep with the TV talking quietly in the background. The house smelled of cigarettes.

The next morning at breakfast, his mom surprised him with a full course meal. He guessed that Aunt Dina had a positive influence on her. They had a pleasant conversation, and everything in Scotch's life felt perfect again. "What are your plans for after school today, son"? He wiped his face with his linen napkin and replied, "I am going to pay a visit to Mrs. Ricker and learn more about that Army Truck. She was going to find the original Owner's Operating Manual. She said that she had a bunch of other stuff from Mr. Ricker's past that would surely interest me. Why do you ask Mom"? She returned to the table and sat beside him. "I would like to take you to a movie sometime. It would be like a date. There will always be another time though. I am so happy that you are taking the time out of your personal life, to help the elderly lady next door. She must be so lonely over there. I bet she loves having you to visit. To me Scotch, that is a very important part of your life, our life. When you grow up as an adult someday, you'll know what I am talking about". "Thanks mom. You and Dad brought me up right, I guess". She stood up and gave him a big hug. He hadn't felt love like that since the night they learned of Mike passing away. "Now brush your teeth and get going to school. You don't want to be late. I'll clean up the kitchen. Do you want me to drive you"? "No, that won't be necessary Mom, I am a grown adult. With a tear in her eye, she replied, "I couldn't agree with you more. If your father was here, he would feel the same way". "Thanks mom, you're the best! I've gone through hell these past six months without him, and you helped me to survive". She chuckled, "That's what mom's are for, and watch your language, young man".

THE END

Printed in the United States
by Baker & Taylor Publisher Services